A HOME WITH DADDY

SERENITY STABLES
BOOK 2

CASSIE HARGROVE

COVER DESIGN BY JM DESIGNS

MODEL: MATTHEW HOSEA

PHOTOGRAPHER: FURIOUSFOTOG

To anyone suffering from mental health, I promise you...
you're not alone!

PREFACE/TRIGGER WARNING

This book deals with the subject of mental health as the FMC has Borderline Personality Disorder.

Not every one person is the same, and if you have questions, or know family and/or friends dealing with BPD, I encourage you to do research on the subject! <3

<u>Triggers:</u>
- Abuse
- PTSD Trauma

CHAPTER 1
RINA

OF COURSE, I WOULD RUN OUT OF MONEY HERE. I absolutely hate small towns and this one screams Podunk.

Why couldn't I have made it to the next city before this happened? It's a lot easier to hide in a sea of people. Not so easy in a small town where everyone knows everyone.

Here, I'm a sitting duck, and I need to get the hell out of Dodge.

Fast.

Only problem is, without money I'm stuck. I will have to try and find a job that pays under the table and a place to stay.

It won't be long before Robert finds me if I stay in one place.

"Fuck!" I pull at the beanie on my head and scream into the night sky. I'm lucky I even made it to this town, really. I've been walking for hours since the last ride I hitched dropped me off miles from anywhere. I wonder what it says about me that I would rather walk in the dead of night with nothing but wild animals and a never-ending road, than to go to the authorities.

Ha. That's fucking laughable.Robert has them firmly in his pocket—going to them for help would only ensure a speedy death..

My granddad passed away when I was sixteen. I always thought Grandma was as healthy as a horse —until she passed away from a heart attack a few months ago. I was safe when she was alive, but due to the trust fund they set up for me, I'm now on the run.

Robert—the ever-loving father he is—wants my money. But my grandparents were smart, ensuring there were rules put into place to prevent him getting his hands on it and squandering it away like he had his own. The only way he can access the money is if I die before turning twenty-five, when the trust becomes accessible to me.

I assume they figured their son wouldn't go so far

as killing his own child. Surely, he had at least a little fatherly love for me, right? Wrong. The only things he cares about are money, maintaining his flashy lifestyle, and appearances.

I just have to evade him and keep myself alive for the next two years. My stomach chooses this moment to growl in pain from hunger. I can't even remember the last time I ate. Or what I ate.

Yikes.

Taking a quick look around me, I see a gas station down the road and make my way there. I'll have to shoplift again. It sucks, sure, but it's the only means of living I have. It's either steal scraps of food where I can, or die from starvation.

I chose to steal, but it's always something small and cheap. A few bags of peanuts here, a couple meat sticks there. I'm doing what I have to do in order to survive until I can come up with a better plan. I'm not an idiot. I know living like this long term is impossible, but I need time.

I've already been living like this for over a couple months, and it hasn't been easy.

Dear old Dad had put on the grieving family schtick for a couple of months before I started noticing things. It started out small. I would feel like

I was being watched and felt paranoid until I saw the same couple of guys around the places I frequented.

Over and over again, they were just there.

It was never at the same time and they always had different disguises, but I'm a paranoid mess so I pay attention to every detail around me.

With each passing day, my anxiety started to pick up more and more until I just never left the house. I didn't know why they were following me, but my gut told me it wasn't anything good.

The only drawback to spending more time at home was being around Robert more. With each passing day his hostility grew, and he would say things to hurt me, to knock me down.

He's never loved me. I don't think he ever really wanted me, but he was stuck with me when my mother ran off before I turned one. I tried really hard to blame her, but as I grew older and saw Robert for who he really was, I couldn't be all that mad at her.

"Good evening miss." A kind older gentleman greets me from behind the register. I give him a small smile. "You're not from around here." It isn't a question—I'm sure I don't dress like anyone he's used to.

My style is eclectic to me. It's a mix of biker chic, bohemian vibes, and some hipster roots.

Yeah, I'm a fucking mess, but I'm okay with that.

"No. I'm just passing through." I fake the largest smile I can muster, and he nods toward me.

Making my way to the back of the store, I start fingering everything and looking around. I can feel the cashier's eyes on me, and I wonder if it's my style or the blue hair that makes him not trust me. Maybe it's just the fact that I'm an outsider.

Small towns are notorious for that. The whole not liking outsiders thing.

Eventually, he turns to do something else, and I sneak a couple packets of peanuts and a few meat sticks into my pockets before he turns back around.

Now that I have what I need, I make a show of going to the cooler to look for a drink and frown. "You don't have any AMP energy drinks?" I turn to him, and he shakes his head.

"Nope. Sorry, darlin', that's not something we carry here. That's more of a city drink."

I groan. Really? Come on! Everyone needs energy boosts every now and then.

"I could never live in a small town. I'd die of caffeine withdrawal," I state as I make my way back up to the front and closer to the door. I don't actually drink caffeine often, but he doesn't know that.

"Why? Plain coffee is just as good." He eyes me for a moment, and I actually gag.

"Yeah, no. I can't stomach coffee. It's just too bitter for me." I give him another smile and back up towards the door with a wave. "Thank you. I'm going to try and get a ride into the city."

I keep walking backwards until I slam into a hard body behind me. I whip around to apologize to the person behind me and freeze.

Shiiiiit. Cops.

Relax and breathe, Rina. It's a small town. He's probably just here to get gas or something. Act normal.

Pfft, that's easy to say when you're not looking at some sort of Adonis. The guy standing before me is easily six feet tall with black hair, jeans, and a beige shirt with his badge attached.

Trailing my gaze from his feet, I notice the cowboy boots he's wearing.

Fucking hell. Cowboy isn't really my thing, but this guy is like an ice cream cone I just want to lick and claim.

Whoa. You really do need to eat if you're comparing a hot guy to food.

I stop my perusal at his deep green eyes and suck

in a breath. Holy shit. He is seriously the hottest guy I have ever seen in my life.

"I am so sorry." My voice comes out more husky than I realized it could sound, and I slap my forehead with the palm of my hand.

"No apology necessary." His deep voice sends a thrill through me. His intense eyes watch me as I swallow and take a breath.

"Alright, well, thank you." I look back over to the cashier and smile. "I'm sorry I bothered you when you don't have what I wanted." He gives me a kind of sad smile before the Adonis' voice sounds again.

"If that's true, then why are you stealing?"

Fuck!

Travis

The girl standing before me looks like she's either going to throw up or start mouthing off at me. I personally don't care which route she chooses, she's still in for a world of trouble.

No one comes into my town, steals from the people just trying to make a living, and gets away with it.

She's short and thin, scarily so. She could most definitely use some food, but she's probably just one of those teenagers thinking they needed to starve themselves to be pretty. I will never understand that mentality. If you're hungry, you eat. It's that simple.

"E—excuse me?" she stammers and swallows, visibly shaking as I stare her down.

Her dark sapphire hair brings out the silver highlights in her brown eyes. If she wasn't a criminal, I might even find her extremely attractive. A little young for me, but it's easy to see the appeal.

"I said, if that's true then why are you stealing from the store?" I can't let myself get lost in her. She's a thief who doesn't belong in my town.

"I—I, uh." She looks between us as guilt crosses her features before taking the meat sticks and peanuts out of her pocket, laying them on the counter. "I'm sorry." She looks to the floor and refuses to meet anyone's eyes and a part of me feels bad for her.

"An apology isn't going to cut it, little girl. You can't just steal things and expect to get away with it. You're going to have to come with me." Shit, why did I call her little girl? That's something I usually reserve for the submissives at the club, not some strange criminal. I need to get my head checked.

8

"That's not really necessary." She straightens her spine, staring at me like her words will make me back down.

Even if she hadn't just tried to steal, I wouldn't be afraid of a little thing like her. "Yes, it is."

She huffs out a breath and rolls her eyes. My palms twitch to spank the sass out of her. It's not something I'm used to feeling towards strangers, but this girl clearly needs direction.

Yeah, and you can't be the one to give it to her.

I didn't say I wanted to be.

Bullshit, Travis. You're dying to discipline this small thing and show her how hot it could be. God, I need to get laid.

"I didn't actually steal it."

I snort and widen my stance. "Because you got caught. Now, we can do this quietly with you following me to the car, or I can cuff you," I tell her.

She sucks in a breath as emotions pass over her face before she locks them up tight so fast, I can't even decipher what they were. "No cuffs," she states, and I nod.

"Then follow me." I hold my hand out towards the door before looking to the owner behind the register. "Thanks for the call, Frank." He nods and thanks me for my help as I'm walking out behind her.

Just before we get to the car, the little minx decides to try and make a run for it, shooting off to the side with more speed than I'd have guessed she had.

Yeah, she definitely needs direction. It's going to be a long fucking night.

CHAPTER 2
TRAVIS

"Let go of me, you jackass," she huffs at me. I haul her back to the car by her arm and put the handcuffs on for good measure.

"Nope, can't, darlin'." I snort at myself because really, she's anything but a darling. Fucking hell, the woman is a menace in my life, and I've only had her around for twenty minutes.

God, all I want to do is go home and relax for the night with a few beers and some quiet.

Quiet where a blue haired pixie demon isn't sassing me.

She's cute though.

"Don't darling me, asshole." She's a fiery one. If she weren't a criminal, I think I could have some serious fun with her and that attitude.

She could use a strong handed Daddy to make her mind.

Who the fuck runs away from a cop in a town where they literally know no one?

When I caught up to her, I ended up tackling her to the ground to get the cuffs on her. She's tiny. Too tiny, like she's been starving herself or something.

"You should really watch the language. Little girls who don't watch their mouths often get them washed out with soap."

Her gasp is almost comical as she narrows her eyes at me, assessing whether or not I would actually do it.

I would. If she were mine, anyway.

"Gross, dude. How old are you? Ninety?" She scoffs at me as I open the cruiser door and help lower her into the back seat before doing up her belt.

"Nope. Just old-fashioned, darlin'." I make sure she's secure in her seat before closing the door at her sounds of complaint.

Oh, she's definitely pissed off with me right now.

It takes less than ten minutes to get to the station and it was spent listening to the girl mutter under her breath while giving me death glares she thinks I didn't notice.

Definitely a wild one.

"Alright, sit here." I guide her to a chair in my office so I can take a seat across from her. "Want to tell me what you're doing in Haven Hills, Ms...?" I trail off, holding my hand out in a gesture for her to tell me her name but she just rolls her eyes at me.

"I'm not telling you my name." That's fine, I can just get her prints instead and run them through the system. I can't imagine a girl like her not having someone worried about her since she's most definitely not from around here.

"We'll table that for now then."

She sighs, leaning back into the chair. "Look, I just wanted some food. I said I was sorry. Can you just let me go now?"

I shake my head. "No, I can't. You can't just get off with a warning when you shoplift. Especially when you won't even tell me your name."

"Because it's not important. Let me go and you will never see me again, alright? I didn't succeed in shoplifting." Something almost sad washes over her face as she looks at the floor and I don't like it.

Fuck knows why I don't like it, but I don't.

"I disagree. Your name is extremely important,

and I will get it by any means necessary." Her already pale face loses some colour it didn't really have to begin with, and I curse myself. "Within legal boundaries, of course." I'm hoping this puts her at ease a bit.

I should word things more carefully in case she's ever been forced into doing something against her will in the past.

"Rina," she whispers so quietly I think I've imagined it. This quiet voice is nothing like the girl who was spitting curse words at me a while ago.

"Rina." Her head bobs before she lifts her gaze. "Thank you for telling me something. I doubt it's your full name, but it's a start." She swallows and nods, a little colour coming back to her cheeks, and I let out a breath. "Can you tell me why you're here? It doesn't seem like somewhere you'd want to be."

Her gaze hardens in a split second and the sassy spitfire is back before I even register what could have tripped the switch.

"I'm sorry, am I too different for this precious hillbilly hellhole?" Definitely struck a nerve.

"Watch the tone and don't be rude." I use my Dom voice on her, hoping she will at least hear the authority in my tone.

"Pfft. Let me go and I won't be rude."

"Not likely to happen when we can't even seem to have a conversation without that mouth of yours running off."

*What the fuck, Travis? Shut the hell up before you get a lawsuit. You're the sheriff and she's a detainee. You're not a Dom with a mouthy Sub at **Ignition**.*

She glares at me wildly as her mouth opens and closes, trying to figure out what to say before she lets out a high growling noise. "Ugh!"

It's actually kind of cute.

Focus!

"Are you going to work with me now, or should I just fingerprint you and give you time to simmer in a cell until you're ready to talk?" Her eyes go wide at that.

I'm not really following protocol with her. I should have gotten her prints first then taken her to the interrogation room, but they're cold to a normal person. She's so damn thin she'd probably freeze to death.

I also figured my office would make her feel safer so she would talk.

"You can't take my prints."

I raise an eyebrow. "I can and I will. I arrested you, darlin'. I have to process you."

She shakes her head violently and flies off her chair.

"No. I am flat out telling you right the fuck now, that you will not get my prints. I refuse to give them to you."

She refuses? She can't just refuse.

"Look, you're young. Maybe you're worried this will show up on college applications, but it's a misdemeanour. It's not going to be that bad, especially if you're not charged."

"This has nothing to do with my age, asshole. I'm twenty-three and I'm refusing to give you my prints, so this is where we come to an end. Kindly, or not so kindly, go fuck yourself!"

Yeah, no. I've had enough of this bullshit for the day. I can deal with her bratty ass tomorrow. Maybe a night in a cell is just the thing she needs to cool off.

"Then I guess you're looking at a night in lock up, darlin'. Let's get you comfy."

That could have gone a lot more smoothly than it did.

The girl has got a set of lungs on her, that's for sure. I have the migraine to fucking prove it.

What the hell is she hiding anyway? It's not normal to flat out refuse to give your prints when you've been arrested. Normally, I would have insisted and forced her to do it, but something about this just feels...wrong.

She's hiding something and I need to figure out what before I can let her go. I refuse to let her cause problems for anyone else in this town.

Not to mention the fact that she's so thin a strong wind would knock her over.

If I step back and look at it rationally, she was stealing yes, but it was meat sticks and peanuts. What if that's all she has been surviving on?

It just isn't sitting right with me, but the girl will not talk to me.

Maybe my deputy Trent would have better luck. Pulling out my phone and thumbing through the contacts until I find him, I hit dial and wait.

"Stevens," he grunts into the phone.

"Hey, are you busy tonight?" Yeah, that was professional. Fuck, I need to sleep.

"Depends. What's going on?" I can hear his

fiancé Lana shuffling in the background, whispering to him. "No, sweet pea, it's Travis."

"I arrested a girl shoplifting from Frank."

"A girl?" Is he deaf?

"Yes, a girl. She's refusing to give me anything, and told me to go fuck myself when I said I would pull her prints." He barks out a laugh and I pinch the bridge of my nose, trying to keep calm.

"That's some serious spunk to throw at a sheriff."

"No shit," I all but growl at him. It's too fucking late for bullshit.

"Okay, what do you need me to do, boss?"

"Want to come down and try speaking to her? Something's not right. I can't put my finger on it, but I could use a second opinion. Maybe a city slicker like you can get her to talk."

He scoffs. "I'm no more of a city slicker than you are, asshole. Yeah, I'll come in. Give me a bit." He hangs up before I can thank him, and I toss my phone on the desk.

CHAPTER 3
RINA

"LET'S GET YOU COMFY," I MUTTER UNDER MY BREATH.
Asshole.

Like I could be comfy in a tiny cell where the
mattress reeks of drunk moron. It's also really cold in
here.

I really fucked up this time, and I have no idea
how I'm going to get myself out of it. I could have let
him take my prints and hoped he let me off with a
warning so I could run, but where would I go? I'm
out of money and living off scraps, practically
starving.

Not to mention, the second my prints hit the
system, Robert would have been on his way here or
sending his goons to kill me.

I should have just ignored my stomach and kept walking. I would have come to another town or store eventually. And if the wild animals got to me first, at least they would make it fairly quick.

Yeah, keep feeling sorry for yourself, Rina. It's exactly what's going to get you out of this mess.

Now I'm stuck here like a sitting duck, and I'm screwed.

I could take the chance and tell the sheriff the truth, but I don't trust cops. Robert has way too many of them in his pocket. Even here, I wouldn't be safe if things were brought to their attention.

Robert wants his money too badly to just let it go.

"Hi, there." A sweet and shy voice pulls me out of my head.

She's a tiny girl like me, but much more clean cut. Kind of a cross between country and chic and she's cute. Adorable even.

What the hell is she doing in here? "Hi?"

She giggles. "Sorry, I'm Lana. Sheriff says your name is Rina?" I narrow my eyes at her trying to see what the hot cop is playing at. There's no way this girl works here.

"Maybe. Who wants to know?" My voice is anything but kind, but she doesn't seem to take it personally. Her face softens as she gives me a small smile, pushing a strand of her long blonde hair behind her ear.

I actually kind of feel like a dick for being so standoffish with her, but what do they expect from me? They locked me in a cell, for crying out loud.

"Just me." Her voice is so quiet and soft. "My fiancé came in to speak to the sheriff, so I figured I would come say hi."

Right. I might be an asshole.

"He didn't send you back here?" I ask, feeling a little mean.

She shakes her head with a smile.

"Nah, he's too protective of his people for that." She giggles again. "Not that you're a danger or anything, he just doesn't know you and I have a bad past." She gets quiet again.

Fuck. Definitely an asshole.

"So, you're from around here?" I ask her, trying to change my irritated tone. It's not her fault I'm on edge and she seems really sweet. The last thing I want to do is hurt her.

"Born and raised. I moved to Omaha for a while, but..." She trails off, and I get the feeling that's the part of her past she was referring to.

"I don't think I could live in a small place like this. I love the noise and energy of the city."

She beams at me. "My fiancé and I did too, but this place has its own kind of energy. The peaceful sounds of nature are kind of amazing and soothing. For me, anyway. I totally understand why you may not think so though."

"So, how come your fiancé is here to talk to the giant ogre?"

She laughs harder at that. "Travis isn't that bad, he's just protective. But Trent is here because he's the deputy." Travis huh? Good to know.

"Damn." Figures the first person to be kind to me would be practically married to a cop.

"What?" She looks genuinely curious as I let out a breath.

"Any secrets on how to get out of here?" I whisper, and she blinks at my change of topic.

"Ummm, I can't think of any, sorry." She looks around like she's trying to find a way to break me out and I laugh. She's so cute. Way too innocent to be caught up in my shit.

"Thanks anyway." I drop back against the wall and sigh as my stomach growls. Fuck, I think I might throw up.

"Are you hungry? I could totally grab you something to eat. What's your favourite food?" Before I can answer, a scarily giant man moves into the room, and I stand up ready to fight him.

He looks like he could kill someone with his bare hands, and if he thinks he's going to hurt my new friend he has another think coming.

"Lana, come stand closer to me." I don't move my eyes off the big man, and she watches me with curious eyes.

"Sweet pea, everything okay in here?" Sweet pea? What kind of a hillbilly nickname is that? Dear Lord, are these men all from a different century?

"Huh? Oh! Everything is fine, D-Sir." She blushes a little before he walks up to her, looking down at her with love and gentleness I wouldn't have expected from a behemoth.

"Is that so?"

She nods and smiles back up at him. "Yep. This is my new friend, Rina!" She's so excited I can't help but fall under her spell a little.

"New friend, huh?" He kisses her head before turning his eyes toward me, assessing me like he's not sure if he can trust me with his girl.

"Hi." I wave shyly, feeling completely awkward. Damn, he's intense.

If I wasn't so damn small, I'd be able to defend

myself better. Definitely need to learn jiu jitsu so I can karate chop anyone's ass.

Wait. That's not right. Whatever, sentiment still applies. Martial arts equals a badass Rina in one tiny lethal package.

I snort to myself before covering my mouth.

"Something funny, little one?" He raises an eyebrow and I look back to Lana.

"This is your fiancé? Is everyone here a giant?" Holy fuck, Rina, shut up.

Lana giggles. "To me? Yes, but I'm tiny. Just like you!"

Trent snorts and shakes his head.

"Alright, sweet pea. I'm going to go back out and talk to the boss man. Come out soon so we can head home. You've had a long day." The way he touches her cheek gently has my heart ready to explode.

I didn't believe love like that existed in the world, but seeing a scary giant being so gentle with someone so tiny? Maybe there's hope in the world after all.

"Promise." She stands on her toes to kiss him before he gives me one last assessing look on his way out.

. . .

Travis

"Everything alright back there?" I ask him when he comes back from checking on Lana.

He's definitely possessive and protective of her, but I don't blame him. When her abusive ex kidnapped her while Trent and her brothers were trying to keep her safe, I could tell he was on the verge of a breakdown. That girl had come to mean something special to him in pretty quick order after the hospital.

"Yeah, she's fine. That girl is pretty jumpy, though." He sits in the seat across my desk, and I grunt. "Tiny too. You need to feed her."

Shit. Food.

I should have gotten her something to eat long before I called Trent. Fuck, I'm a dick.

"I'll order something now." Pulling my phone out, I send a text to Sammi. She's a nice woman who runs the pizza shop down the street. They're technically closed, but I know she'll do this for the station.

"You don't seem like yourself, man. What's going on?" he questions.

I groan and run my hands over my face. "I honestly don't know. I'm just tired."

He nods, watching me. "Then ask Ethan to come in an hour early and go home. He won't care." I wince.

How the fuck am I supposed to explain to him that my gut is screaming at me to never leave her side? That something is wrong, and she needs protection and I have to be the one to give it to her?

It sounds insane. It has to be the Daddy Dom in me seeing her as a quiet submissive in need of help.

I snort at myself. Quiet, my ass. I can still feel the migraine in my temples. "I can't. Don't ask."

He watches me, the corner of his mouth ticking up and shrugs.

"That's not like you, Travis. Getting all edgy about a detainee." The need to strangle him is high at the moment. I hate when he plays these games.

"Nothing odd about it when it's not old man Dave sleeping it off in the cell again. She's not from around here and my gut is telling me she's hiding a whole lot." It's the truth. We don't have many arrests here that aren't just the locals being a little too rowdy sometimes. Haven Hills is a quiet town.

It just so happens my instincts also seem to be screaming at me to not leave her alone and I need to know why.

Maybe I just need a night at *Ignition* to let my Dom side out for a scene or two. *Ignition* is a BDSM club a friend of mine from high school started about ten years ago. Back then, BDSM wasn't as widely known or accepted, so the club was the perfect way to be yourself.

I remember when Archer first asked me if I wanted to join him in training and I thought he was insane, but I went anyway. Turns out, the Dom training was what I had been craving my entire life, and now I was able to do that safely with any submissive.

It was an extensive six-month training program that he's now recreated for his own club. If you're new to the lifestyle, you're able to take the training to learn everything you need about how to be a good Dom or submissive.

"I think you're lying. Maybe even to yourself."

Lana comes back out and stops beside Trent.

"Umm." She twiddles her fingers in front of her and bites her lip, completely nervous—which sets me on edge.

"Lana, speak up." Trent uses his Dom voice and I'm always impressed with how good he is with her.

He's always had a reputation for being a hardass.

You don't get to be a top detective in the city without being intense.

"Right, sorry." She swallows. "Sir, Sheriff… could I please grab something out of Rina's bag?"

I lift an eyebrow at her. "No." She lets out a huff, stomping her foot and Trent has to cover his amusement.

"That's not fair. You don't even know what I want to get from it." Her hands are on her hips, and I shoot Trent a stunned look. He's just going to let her brat out at me then? Lovely.

"If Rina would like something, she can ask me. It is not your job to do so." She blushes and looks completely uncomfortable which has Trent sitting up straight and alert.

"With all due respect, Sheriff." She looks at Trent and swallows before looking at me again. Oh, I'm not going to like this. "You're being a rude meanie! I wouldn't ask if it wasn't something important."

"Now, you hang on a minute here. You don't get to talk to me like that, Lana." Trent moves forward on his chair and growls at me, making me wince. "Sorry."

"No. I'm sorry, it's just really really important," Lana whispers, looking dejected.

I sigh and look from her to Trent. He's not happy

with me for losing my cool on her and I don't want to piss him off.

"What is it and I will get it." She looks completely nervous, and bends down to whisper in Trent's ear. His face goes from amused to complete shock and then understanding.

"Mind if I get it out? It really is personal, and I technically work here, so no chain of evidence will be broken."

What are they playing at? I narrow my eyes between them before sighing and pointing to her bag in the corner. It doesn't take Trent long to find whatever it is, and he takes off his hoodie, wrapping it up to hide from me before passing it to Lana.

Once she thanks us, she heads back to the holding cells, and I'm dumbfounded.

"Going to tell me what that was now that Lana is gone?"

He shakes his head. "Nope. Sorry, boss. I can't on this one, but I promise you it's important and she can't use it to escape with."

Lana comes back just as Sammi walks in with the pizza, a huge smile on her face.

I'm not an idiot. I know she has a thing for me and she's sweet, but she's just not my type.

"Oh good. She's totally starving and needs food. My tummy hurts just listening to hers grumble," Lana says, and I feel a pang of guilt in my chest.

She really was stealing that food because she was starving. "Did she tell you anything?"

She shrugs and looks at me.

"Sorry, not really. And anything she does tell me is one hundred percent girl code, boss man."

"Lana, this could be a matter of safety." She goes pale and I curse myself. I'm just fucking up with her all around tonight, aren't I?

"I know. I didn't get any of that kind of information from her. We just talked about some other things, but I get the impression she's scared."

"Lana, are you okay?" She nods, tears brimming in her eyes as Trent wraps her up in his arms, pulling her into his lap.

It shouldn't be a time for me to be jealous, but I am. He found his own Little and was living the dream life I have always wanted.

Sammi knocks on the office door with a smile, and I give her a small one back, getting up to meet her. I quickly explain to her that I have a lot of work to do and a meeting with Trent to get back to.

I don't want to tell her I arrested someone and have the girl being judged before I can even get some answers. Frank is a solid guy. He won't mention it to anyone for a while.

She apologizes, kissing my cheek before wishing us all a goodnight.

"I'm fine, I can just tell, you know? I can tell she's scared about something, and I don't think it has anything to do with being locked up." Trent curses as I set the pizza on my desk and sit back down.

Of course, she would know all about being scared and in danger. It wasn't too long ago her abusive and psychotic ex was stalking her.

"Okay, thank you for telling me. That was really good, Lana, I appreciate it." I can tell she's withdrawn into little space just by watching her. She's more antsy and pulled into herself, her eyes avoiding anyone but Trent's. It's not the first time I've seen her in little space, and I'm sure it won't be the last.

"I'm going to take her home. Don't forget to feed that girl." I nod as he stands, carrying Lana in his arms and I try to not let the jealousy of his situation eat me alive.

After they're gone, I grab two plates and throw a couple slices of pizza on each before grabbing a couple bottles of water out of the mini fridge in my office.

It's time to see if I can be someone other than the asshole who arrested her.

CHAPTER 4
RINA

I DIDN'T SLEEP LAST NIGHT. I ATE WAY TOO MUCH pizza and spent most of the night in pain.

I know I looked like a pig, but I was starving, and I have no clue when I will get to eat again. I never do. So, when I'm given food, I eat as much as I can so my body has as much fuel as I can give it.

I can already feel the stress and anxiety increasing the longer I'm here. I haven't stayed in one place this long in almost two months, always on the move and never staying in one spot. It makes it harder to track me down.

The only saving grace I may have is being locked in this cell so they can't readily find me. Or at least, not access me as easily. Not without killing the sheriff and even Robert wouldn't be able to get himself out of something like that.

Right?

I squeeze my stuffed robot, Circuit, tighter against me as I face the wall and try to go back to sleep. I know it seems childish to sleep with stuffies, but I've had him for years and I legitimately cannot sleep without him.

I was terrified to ask Lana for him, but she had mentioned her own stuffed butterfly and it made my chest ache knowing he was within reach but I couldn't have him.

Eventually I asked her, and she smiled her bright and sweet smile at me before leaving me alone. When she came back, she had Circuit rolled up in her fiancé's sweater, so I knew she hadn't told the sheriff about him.

I'm not sure how he would react to me having a stuffed robot so I will continue to keep it hidden until I can get out of here. The last thing I need is some country bumpkin asshole judging me for the one and only crutch I have.

"Time to wake up." I hear his voice from the door and groan.

"No." I really don't want to get up unless he's letting me leave. "Unless you're letting me leave?" I can't hide the hopefulness in my voice, and he snorts.

"Yeah, that's not happening." Ugh! Why the fuck not? I want to stomp my foot and throw something at him, but the only thing I have readily available is Circuit and my pillow. Neither of which I'm willing to give up.

Besides, I could never throw Circuit. It would hurt him.

"Are you going to give me the correct information I need to process you? If you do, then I can release you. Maybe." Maybe, my ass. And there's no way I can give him my real information.

They're probably already hot on my trail and if I give the sheriff my info now, I will never get away from them in time.

"I can't do that, so I guess I'll just go back to sleep."

"Not the way it works, little girl. Come on." Ugh, would he stop calling me little girl? I know I'm short and small, but geez.

"You know I'm not that small, right? Just because every guy in this town is a behemoth doesn't mean I'm tiny," I grumble, getting out of bed and being careful to hide Circuit beneath the covers.

"Did you just call me a behemoth?" He looks dumbstruck when I turn around and I smile.

"You betcha, Sheriff. Now, why do I have to get up?"

He unlocks the cell door and holds it open.

"Come have breakfast with me in my office. You need to eat."

I scoff at him while looking between the bed and the open door. Will Circuit be safe here?

"Will you lock up the cell while I'm with you?" He lifts an eyebrow but gives me a sharp nod.

"Sure. Not sure why you want that, but I assume it's whatever Lana helped you hide?" I blush and nod, looking at the floor as I move past him, waiting while he locks up again before guiding me back to his office.

If he keeps feeding me like this, I won't be staying tiny for long. Geez, has the man never heard of healthy food? The pizza last night was awesome and so were the pancakes this morning, but holy hell. Talk about a carb overload.

Then again, looking at him I can tell he takes health seriously. How could he not when he's so freaking muscular and huge?

Which means one thing. He's trying to give me a sense of security to make me trust him. If only he knew that feeding me carbs wasn't even close to getting me to trust someone.

"Thank you for breakfast." I sigh, leaning back in my chair. "And dinner last night. But you can't keep me here forever."

He nods, watching me closely. "You're right, I can't. But I can't let you go either." I narrow my eyes and growl at him in frustration. What the hell is with his insistent need to keep me here?

You'd think he would want a criminal out of his town.

"That's called kidnapping."

He snorts. "It's called knowing you're hiding something and being worried about you." I swallow. Worried about me? No one has been worried about me Not since my grandparents died.

Between Robert royally fucking up my child-hood and my mother abandoning me, I was diagnosed with Borderline Personality Disorder, or BPD for short, by the time I was sixteen.

I can't bring myself to trust anyone, especially strangers.

If you wanted to be close to me, it would take time. That goes for anyone, and if you ever broke that trust? Well, you'd never earn it back. I would always second guess your true intentions and motives for everything.

It's impossible for him to be worried about someone he doesn't know who also happens to be on the opposite side of the law. Not that I choose to be there.

I'm not really a criminal, I'm just doing what I have to in order to survive.

"You can't care about me," I spit out before I think better of it, and he raises an eyebrow. Dammit, why is everything he does so hot and infuriating at the same time?

"And why is that?" I blink, my mouth opening and closing a few times while my brain tries to play catch up. Damn him and his good looks for distracting me. He gives me a smirk and I feel the annoyance creeping back in.

Good. Annoyance I can work with. Attraction, I can't. "Because!"

He chuckles. "That's really not an answer, little

girl." More growling from me. He really needs to stop fucking calling me little!

"I'm not little!" He just smiles.

"You are too. I could carry you around on my hip all day and wouldn't even feel you there."

"Like hell you could!" I stammer and his grin gets wider.

"I most definitely could, but we aren't there yet." He clears his throat and sits up. "Look, I know you're hiding something, and I don't think it's a criminal record. Until you tell me the truth, you will be attached to me at the hip. Wherever I go, you go."

"You've lost your mind, old man. Better start taking some omega-3's before it deteriorates further."

The smile drops off his face and I smile in satisfaction. Not that I will admit it to anyone, but it's kinda fun to get under his skin.

"I'm not that old, and you may want to watch your mouth, girl."

I scoff. "Or what? You can't do shit." Oh. Oh, I so don't like the look he has right now. It's a look of complete control. My grandpa used to get that look before he would swat my ass for swearing when I was a kid. Not that it helped.

Obviously.

I just stopped swearing when he was in earshot, but no way in hell am I backing down from this.

Crossing my arms over my chest, I stare him down without flinching.

I will win this one way or another.

CHAPTER 5
TRAVIS

POOR THING IS DEFINITELY RATTLED.

After breakfast we had what could only be described as a nonverbal standoff. Me insisting she stay with me until she tells me the truth and her trying to refuse.

I say trying because she's currently in the front seat of my truck, glaring at the passing scenery as if it's somehow offended her.

I don't know her story or what is happening with her life, but I do know I can't just let her go. My gut is telling me she needs help and I have to be the one to help her.

I battled with my rational side all night on whether she would be safest with me or if I should leave her with the Easton brothers.

They're extremely protective of women and children, and their ranch, Serenity Stables, is currently in the middle of being converted to a sort of safe house for victims who need to disappear. Lana came up with the concept a year ago when her ex almost killed her during a beating. After she moved home, she dealt with his stalking and kidnapping her before I ultimately killed him to save her life.

She decided she wanted to go to college to become a counsellor to help other victims. Hell, she's now working alongside my little brother Derek so they can offer his psychiatry services as well as her training.

Derek still lives in Kansas City, Kansas, but he's been amazing with video calls and helping Lana accept and move past her trauma and that's exactly what they want to offer others.

It didn't take them long to convince myself and the captain of the Omaha police department to work together to create that type of environment and it should be up and running within the next few months.

So, yeah. I could have left her in the Easton's capable hands, especially given my deputy, Trent Stevens, also lives on the property due to his engagement to Lana. She may be the littlest Easton sibling, but she's quite possibly the fiercest.

But I couldn't do it.

Not after going to check on her in the middle of the night and seeing her asleep with a tattered stuffed robot tight against her chest and sucking on her thumb. My protective Daddy instincts took over and leaving her with anyone else suddenly wasn't an option.

She was so damn cute sucking on her thumb and cuddling that robot that I just wanted to wrap her up in my arms and hold her close until she knew she was safe here. That she could trust me.

"Are you sure you're not taking me to some abandoned field to murder me?"

What the fuck?

I side eye her, trying to assess if she's joking but she's still looking out the window. I'd like to think she's joking, but what if she's not? What if she really thinks someone wants to kill her?

Do they?

I feel my blood starting to boil and I grip the steering wheel hard, trying to catch my breath.

"No murderous intent from me, Pixie. Sorry if you're disappointed."

She scoffs before going quiet. "Pixie?"

I smile a little, giving her a quick look and a wink.

"Sure. After you ran from me last night when I tried to bring you in, my first thought was about you being some sort of blue-haired pixie demon." I shrug and she gapes at me before huffing.

"That is beyond rude!"

I chuckle, shaking my head at her little outburst as I turn into my driveway.

I live about fifteen minutes outside of the town limits. Far enough away for privacy, but close enough to get there quickly in an emergency and it's perfect. I've never been one for the sounds and smells of the city or even living directly in town. I enjoyed my privacy and the sounds of nature to sooth me after a long day of work.

"Whoa," I hear her whisper under her breath, but I don't say anything. If she had wanted me to actually hear her, she would have spoken a little louder. I won't pretend that it didn't make my chest swell with pride though.

This place is my sanctuary, my oasis. She's actually the only person I've ever brought out here.

Lots of people know my address, but they respect

my wishes of being left alone when I'm not in uniform. It's something I love about our little town. Everyone respects everyone.

Once I've parked the truck by the door, I shut it off before turning towards her.

"There are going to be rules."

She groans, pouting a little and it's so fucking cute I want to reach over and pinch her lip, but I don't.

I wonder if she even realizes she's a Little. She doesn't seem the type that would be ashamed of anything she did or felt if she was confident in it.

No, after the way she was too embarrassed to let me see the robot, I think she's ashamed of those parts of her and keeps them hidden.

In that case, she probably feels like there is something wrong with her instead of realizing that it's not all that uncommon to be a Little and she's not alone. I'd love to help her navigate that, but her safety comes first.

"Always keep the doors and windows locked. If you get too hot, the house has central air for every room. I don't like being hot either." She blinks and gives me a little smirk. I'd love to know what's running through her mind right now.

"Okay." She nods, her eyes never leaving mine. Good girl.

Fuck, slow down, man.

"You don't go anywhere alone." She goes to speak, and I hold my hand up. "It's not that I don't trust you, though that's up for debate until you can be honest with me." She winces a little and I feel a bit guilty, but I don't back down. "Not only do I believe you're on the run from something or someone that you're afraid of, but there are wild animals here that could eat you alive."

She whimpers and tears brim her eyes.

Taking off my seatbelt, I slide across the bench seat to gently lift her chin so she's looking into my eyes.

"You're safe with me, Rina. I won't let anything happen to you. I know whatever is going on in that adorable head of yours is scary and it will take time for you to trust me, but can you try?" Her eyes move between mine as she exhales a sharp, wobbly breath.

"I can try," she whispers, and I nod.

"Good girl. That's really good." Her body seems to relax into my touch at the praise and I make a mental note to remember that in the future.

"Your health and safety come first while you're in my care." She nods. "That means we will be going to see Doctor Evans first thing in the morning to get you looked over."

She gasps and fire heats her eyes.

"I don't fucking think so! I hate doctors. I'm fine. Besides, I can't exactly afford to pay for a doctor when I can't even pay for meat sticks and peanuts."

She has a point, but the cost doesn't matter. "It's taken care of."

She narrows her eyes at me. "If you mean that you're paying, then absolutely not. I refuse to be a burden to you."

I snort, barely talking myself out of mussing up her hair underneath the hat she's wearing.

"I would pay to make sure you were healthy if I had to, but I don't. Doc has a soft spot for anyone who needs help."

"I don't need to see the damn doctor," she growls, and I growl back.

"Yes, you do. I'd venture a guess you weigh maybe one hundred pounds and haven't been eating. You will get checked so I can make sure to help you get better." She huffs out a breath looking like she wants to fight, but ultimately gives in. "Good. Now, is there anything else about your medical history I should know in case something happens?"

She looks uneasy, moving her eyes away from me to look out the windshield. I can feel the nervousness running off her as she vibrates in the passenger seat.

"Um...you may, uh..." She starts biting her thumb nail and I put a stop to that right away. That's a bad nervous habit to have. I had a buddy when I was younger that would chew on his nails so much his fingertips would bleed because he just couldn't stop.

I don't want to see her working herself up that badly. "You can tell me, Pixie. I promise not to judge you or make fun of you."

She whimpers and nods, knotting her hands together.

"I uh, have Borderline Personality Disorder," she rushes out on a large breath.

"Okay? Do you feel up to telling me what that means?" She looks at me like I've grown a third head before her eyes well up with tears again.

"You're not making me?"

I sigh and shake my head while giving her the gentlest smile I can. "No. If you don't want to tell me, I just ask that you tell Doctor Evans tomorrow."

She takes another deep breath.

"No one has ever given me a choice before." I see red. I'm so angry at anyone and everyone from her past for forcing her into things, that I may actually kill them if I could get my hands on them.

It's never okay to force anyone into something, but it's doubly not okay to make someone fear speaking.

"It's okay, please don't get angry." Her voice breaks, bringing me out of my head and back to the present.

"Never."

She scoffs, looking at me like I'm crazy. "You can't promise that."

"Look at me, Pixie." I pull her chin up again so she pays attention to what I'm about to tell her. "I won't ever get angry with you. I may get upset or frustrated sometimes, but I won't ever use anger towards you. Not ever."

I watch the different emotions cross her face, even spotting a small glimmer of hope before her mask is back up.

"You're making it sound like this is a permanent thing. I assure you it's not." She glares at me and opens the door, jumping out before turning back to me. "BPD is an emotional disorder that is caused by childhood trauma. It makes me moody, depressed, and anxious. It also means I don't trust you and likely won't be here long enough to even try. And I don't get close to people. The end." She slams the door and I'm left with my mouth hanging open in shock at being dismissed as I watch her waltz to the front door and wait for me.

CHAPTER 6
RINA

I'M TRYING TO NOT FALL ASLEEP. IF I CAN OUTLAST him, I can try and run while he's snoring away. If he even snores. Be kind of a shame if he did though.

I actually feel uneasy about bolting on him after he brought me into his home, gave me some track pants and a shirt to shower and change into, and a place to sleep. But I can't stay here.

My heart and mind are already trying to cling to the sheriff and this town because he, Lana, and her behemoth fiancé have been super nice to me the past twenty-four hours.

I'm doing it for their own good though. They don't need baggage like mine hanging around and bringing danger to their quiet little town.

I basically knew I was screwed when I told him

the one thing he could use against me if he wanted to. I told him about my BPD and how vulnerable it makes me.

If he were to do research, he could really hurt me if I stuck around. Not that I think he would, unless he's like the guys on Robert's payroll, but he feels different.

He feels true and strong. Old-fashioned and protective and for some reason he wants to protect me.

I don't get it.

After about an hour of waiting, hearing absolutely nothing in the house, I decide to make my move.

Tiptoeing to the door, I open it as quietly as possible before sticking my head out and looking to see if there are signs of life.

When I'm convinced I can do this, I quietly start heading towards the door.

"And where do you think you're going?"

I scream, jumping so high I fall on my ass on the way down.

"Oopmh." My heart races as the light in the living room turns on and he moves to tower over me. "Are you trying to kill me too? God!" I screech, and then slap a hand over my mouth.

"Too?" His face is thunderous, and I close my eyes. "And don't even think about lying to me, Pixie girl. I will tan your hide if you do."

Oh, he didn't. "You...you can't...WHAT?!"

He smirks down at me, his eyes dark and I shiver. I'm not afraid of him, not really. I don't feel like he would ever harm me, but then again, he did just threaten to spank me.

Me! A grown ass woman. Who the hell does he think he is?

"You can't just threaten to spank me. I'm a grown woman, asshole. God! Are all you men behemoths? Can you back up, please? You're freaking me out."

He winces before taking a few steps back and I feel like I can breathe again. "I can and will tan your hide for lying to me. I don't tolerate liars."

I narrow my eyes at him. "No way are you ever laying a hand on my butt." I groan. Fuck, I can't even seem to curse at him right now. I'm too discombobulated.

"We'll see. Want to tell me why you asked if I was trying to kill you *too*?" I wince.

Yeah, way to let that slip, Katrina, geez.

"Fine. Yes, someone is trying to kill me. No, I'm not crazy and no, I won't tell you about it."

"And why the hell not?" he growls, and I try not

to flinch. Dude is way too much of a giant to be so growly. He's like a growly lion.

"Because I have it handled." I nod, crossing my arms over my chest. I must look ridiculous sitting on the floor on my bruised ass, trying to be stern but I don't care.

"You have it handled," he repeats, and I nod. "Does starving yourself count as having it handled?"

I open and close my mouth until I'm fuming.

"Don't judge me, you...you ogre!" His lips thin, trying to hide his amusement, and it makes me even madder. "You're a giant behemoth ogre who is super mean!"

No. No way, Katrina. Reel that mental shit back in. This is not the time to have a nervous breakdown and let your psycho out.

"A giant behemoth ogre. Who is super mean," he repeats again and I huff, throwing my hands in the air.

"Are you just going to repeat everything I say?"

He lets one side of his mouth curl up. "Depends. Are you going to tell me why you're in danger?"

There's no way he's letting me out of this without some form of truth. I can tell him bits and pieces, but not enough to give him an idea of who I am.

"I have a trust fund that I come into in two years.

Someone wants it, and the only way they can access it is to kill me. So, I ran instead." Instead of anger, he looks almost fearful before taking a few steps over to me and kneeling on the ground, so we are face to face.

"How long have you been running all alone, Pixie?" His voice is so soft I feel the tears building again.

Ugh, why can't he just be a super mean uncaring ogre instead of being a big friendly giant ogre that seems to care? He's sliding past all of my well-crafted walls like they don't even exist, and I don't know how to feel about it.

"A couple months." I don't look him in the eyes, and he curses softly before pulling me into his chest and holding me tight.

Whoa, wait. Abort, you don't like touch.

But it feels so nice and safe.

"I'm so sorry you've been on the run and trying to survive all alone for the past couple months, Pixie. God, that's so not okay." His voice actually hitches, and I wonder if he's crying too, but that can't possibly be right. "Let me help you. Let me help keep you safe," he begs.

"Okay," I give in, unwilling to really fight him anymore. He's managed to make me feel more wanted in one day than I have for most of my life. Maybe I'm crazy for giving in, but I'm so tired.

"Thank you. We will figure this out, Rina, I promise." I swallow, nodding against his chest as he holds me tight. I want to believe him, but I know this won't last.

Eventually Robert will find me and kill me. But maybe, just maybe, I can remember what it's like to be happy for a little while before then.

Travis

Seeing her sitting on the floor and hearing some of her story breaks my heart.

God, what I wouldn't give to destroy the person or people responsible for her fearing for her safety, her life.

I can't believe she's been running on her own for months now. No one to watch out for her or make sure she's eating. No one to keep her safe.

There's only so much you can do while on the run.

She can't get a job without giving up her name, which means not being able to get food without having to steal it. I don't even want to think about how she kept clean or where she may have slept. I'm bound to go on a killing spree if I do.

I hate that she's been going through this alone and I almost treated her like just another criminal.

Isn't that what you did though? You sure as hell weren't very nice to her, asshole.

Fuck.

"I'm sorry, Pixie," I whisper into her hair once she calms down a little. She pulls her head back to look me in the eye, the question evident on her face. "I'm sorry I didn't even stop to give you a chance to explain yourself."

She scoffs, shaking her head.

"You gave me plenty of opportunities, I just didn't trust you. I'm still not sure if I can." My heart aches just hearing her say that. How long has it been since she's been able to trust someone?

I know she said she has Borderline Personality Disorder and I've already emailed my brother for some more information so I can better know what I'm dealing with. He said he would get back to me with the information as fast as he could.

I didn't tell him why I needed it, but he knows not to ask questions in my line of work, just like I know not to ask about his. Confidentiality is iron clad unless someone is in danger.

Technically, Rina is in danger, but not in the way that Derek could ever help.

No, it's up to me to help her and I'm not stopping until she feels safe.

"I still could have been less....cold to you." I'm not proud of how I acted. Even if she did steal, I was a hardass and I feel like shit because of it.

"Is that what you're calling it? Cause I call it being an ass." She sticks her tongue out at me with a grin.

Oh, the little brat.

"Is that so?" I watch her face blush, but she doesn't back down.

"Yep!" Her voice is going a bit higher which is a sure sign she's going into little space.

If her adorable tantrum on the floor hadn't been enough of a clue, this would have solidified it for me. Not that I would ever admit that it's adorable for her to throw a tantrum.

Now the question is: How do I broach the subject, or should I even try?

I doubt she's looking for different ways to accept herself right now with everything else going on.

"And what do you think I should do about that,

Pixie girl?" She sucks in a breath as her eyes go wide and it takes me a second to even realize what I said to cause that reaction. "Shit. I'm sorry."

She shakes her head. "No, it's okay. I actually liked it." She watches my face a moment as I smile down at her in my lap before leaning into me. "Can I tell you a secret?" Her voice is a loud whisper, like a little kid who thinks they're being quiet when they aren't. I lean down just as conspiratorially and whisper.

"Sure, Pixie girl. What's the secret?" She giggles and everything in me feels like I've won something big because I'm the one that got her to let her walls down. It's such an adorable sound and something tells me she doesn't laugh often.

"I actually like it here. But shhhh…" She holds her finger to her mouth. "You can't tell anyone!"

"And why can't I tell anyone?" I whisper back, as seriously as I can muster.

"Because, dude! This place is like suuuupppper Podunk."

Well now. I actually take offence to that.

"Excuse you, Pixie, but this is a very nice town, thank you very much!" I pretend to be outraged, and she giggles before a giant yawn escapes. "Alright, I think it's time for you to sleep."

She pouts at me. "Nooo. I don't wanna." I shake my head, moving us around until I can stand up with her in my arms, grabbing her bag as I go. "EEEK!" Her arms fly around my neck as she closes her eyes so hard, I think it may actually be hurting her.

"I've got you, don't worry," I whisper, my grip tightening around her as I make my way back to the spare room.

It's never been used, and I honestly don't know why I even set it up as a spare room when I don't have anyone over. Though, when I built the cabin, I knew I would want a forever Little someday and wanted to give her a playroom. As far as kids, well, if we chose to have any, building onto the cabin would be a piece of cake.

Setting her onto the bed, I bend down to remove her shoes while she glares at me. "Have you lost your mind?!"

I raise an eyebrow at her dramatics. "Uh, no?"

She scoffs. "You can't just go picking a girl up without warning. Geez, I swear you're all about giving me a heart attack tonight!"

And I swear her Little is very over dramatic.

"You're right. I will warn you next time."

"Next time?"

I shrug, looking up at her after taking her shoes off.

"Never know when I'm going to have to carry a little girl, now do I?" She narrows her eyes at me, and I smile. I know she hates being called little, but seeing that brattiness in her makes me feel proud.

Don't ask me why. It makes absolutely no sense, but it's the truth.

I never thought brats were my thing before, but she's already proving me wrong about that. Or maybe it's just her.

"You are incouragallle." She yawns halfway through telling me off, and I can't hold in the chuckle.

"And you're cute." I boop her nose and she sighs.

Shit.

Did I just call her cute? What if she doesn't like that coming from a complete stranger?

"Meanie."

I shake my head, smiling more than I have in a long time and stand up. "Time for sleep. Is your robot in the bag?" Her eyes go wide again, and I could kick myself for bringing that up. I'm not supposed to know about it.

"You know about Circuit?" she screeches, and it's so cute I would smile if she didn't look so mortified.

Circuit. That's actually a really good name.

Fuck, everything about Rina is cute.

"Uh, yeah." I wince, rubbing the back of my neck. "I went to check on you in the middle of the night and you were sleeping facing the door with him against your chest."

She groans, looking absolutely mortified before her head flies up.

"Was I doing anything else?" She's panicking and I don't like it.

"No, Pixie." She lets out a long breath as her shoulders deflate.

I'm not about to tell her I saw her sucking her thumb when she's on the verge of panicking over something as simple as a stuffie. And I'm sure as hell not going to tell her I thought it was adorable.

She's silent for a second before looking at her bag longingly, and I wish I could help her accept this part of herself. Help her to know it's alright to accept who you are no matter what.

"It's okay to sleep with a stuffie at night, you know. Lots of adults do it," I promise her, and the look she gives me says she doesn't believe me.

"It's childish." She's so quiet that I almost don't hear her. I decide to try a different tactic.

"What made you comfortable with telling Lana

about Circuit last night?"

She purses her lips together. "She mentioned her stuffed butterfly."

I nod in understanding. "And do you think Lana is childish?"

She gasps then looks away, blushing. "No. She's the nicest person I've ever met."

I give her a small smile. "So, why would you think it's childish for one and not the other?"

She shrugs but refuses to look at me. She does follow my movements as I open her bag to give her the stuffy in question though.

"There's a lot about me you don't know." She takes Circuit and holds him tight. At least I think it's a him. It's blue and grey and Circuit doesn't seem like a girl robot name.

"I hope to get to know all of you." She doesn't say anything, sadness written all over her face.

"I'm really tired. Would it be alright if I went to sleep now?"

I nod, not wanting to push her too hard too fast. "Of course. I will just be in the living room if you need anything." I walk to the door, looking back as she gets under the covers, the robot tight against her chest. "Goodnight, Rina."

"Night."

CHAPTER 7
RINA

How the fuck did I let that happen last night? I have never once let another person see that side of me. The crazy, mentally deprived part. God, he must think I'm a complete whack job after acting like a child last night. I'll give him props though, he took it in stride and didn't seem to be bothered by it.

At one point it felt like he was even playing along, but that has to be my fucked up brain talking. There's no way a sexy older man like him could ever find a grown woman acting like a child, normal.

I've barely spoken a word to him this morning as he made me eat oatmeal and fruit. Gag, I hate oatmeal, but the sneaky bastard stirred my fruit in with the gross goo, so I had no choice but to swallow down some of it.

He's tried to get me engaged in conversation all morning, but I can't even look him in the eye. I'm beyond disgusted with myself, and I'd rather curl into a ball alone than be sitting in a doctor's waiting room.

"Pixie, you alright?" I shrug, still refusing to look at him. Why does he care so much?

The second the doctor walks in he's probably going to tell him I'm a complete nut job that needs to be locked away in an institution.

Wouldn't that just be great? Robert would be able to hire a nurse to dose me wrong and then it's 'Bye Bye, Rina'.

"Little girl, you will talk to me after this appointment is over." He practically growls at me, and I roll my eyes.

"Stop pretending to actually care. It's bullshit." He goes to stand up but stops when the door opens, and a man walks in wearing a white lab coat.

Goody, a doctor.

"Sheriff." I watch him nod at Travis respectfully, before closing the door and turning to me. "And you must be Rina."

I snort, my attitude in full force now. "Good guess, Doc. Did the hair give it away?" He looks a little shocked that I spoke to him so rudely, but I can't stop. "Or was it the fact that I have a vagina?"

Travis growls again before moving to squat in front of me. "Pix, I swear to God, if you don't control that mouth of yours, you're going to be sorry."

"Whatever." It's not like he's going to do anything to me, they're just empty threats. He'd actually have to give a shit about me in order to act on his words.

I can see his jaw working as he tries hard not to act on his anger, and his words from yesterday come back to me.

I promise I will never get angry at you. I may get annoyed or frustrated, but it will never ever be directed at you.

I wish more than anything that I could believe him, but he will have to earn my trust before I believe it. Everyone has a temper.

Case in point. Me right now.

The doc looks between us in confusion for a moment before clearing his throat. "Alright, let's move on to the appointment, yeah?" I just barely stop myself from rolling my eyes before giving him a nod and his shoulders seem to relax.

If I were in a better headspace, I could acknowledge I'm being a bitch, but I'm not. They're stuck with bitchy Rina today and they'll just have to deal with it.

"Okay." He smiles, sitting down in a chair. "The sheriff mentioned that you haven't been eating much recently and that he's concerned for your health." I glare at Travis, and he shrugs unapologetically.

"I won't apologize for caring about your well-being." Again, with this caring bullshit.

"Before we go any farther, Rina, I need to know if you want the sheriff to wait outside." My eyebrows shoot up to my hairline, not expecting that to be an option at all and apparently Travis doesn't think so either.

"Like hell!"

The doctor sighs. "Sheriff, even you are aware that detainees still have access to confidentiality, and given you brought her here from your home and not the station, I'm going to guess she's not really a detainee." Well now I feel smug as shit.

"You mean not everyone just bows down to the great Sheriff Travis?" The doctor lets out a snort before Travis glares at him.

"Not when it comes to my license and the oath I took. Would you like him to leave while we go through your appointment?" I smirk at Travis until I can see his blood almost boiling and then shake my head.

"No, it's fine. He can stay."

He looks at me for a moment. "Are you sure that's alright?"

I shrug. "Yeah, it's fine. I just needed him to see that I owned his balls in that moment. He has a big head on him if you haven't noticed." His eyes go wide before he focuses on the papers on his desk, trying to hide his smile and wisely ignoring the sheriff.

Fuck, it's fun to rile him up. I feel better already.

Well, mostly. I still hate myself a little.

"Okay, Rina. If the sheriff didn't mention it, my name is Doctor Evans, but you're welcome to call me Richard if that helps the anxiety of being around a new person." Aww, he's actually kind of sweet. I think about telling him that, but Travis is glaring at the doc like he wants to strangle him and it's hard to keep a straight face.

Someone pissed in his cornflakes this morning.

Also, gross. I hate cornflakes.

"Doctor Evans is fine." I give him a small smile and hope that Travis will ease the hell up because he has a vein in his neck that looks ready to blow.

Can someone survive a neck vein blowing? Is

that a thing? I think I saw something similar on *Grey's Anatomy* once, but that was a fragile and thin vein. There is nothing fragile about the good sheriff.

We make it through the rest of the appointment on basically friendly terms, aside from him sticking me with a damn needle for blood work.

Needles are really scary.

Travis was great though, like he could pick up on my fear and anxiety and gave me his hand, telling me I could squeeze as hard as I wanted to, and you better believe I did. When we were finished, he had an outline of every finger on his hand.

Poor guy.

"Hey, Doc." Travis stops him before he gets up and I groan. Dammit, I just want out of this torture chamber they call an office!

"Yeah?" Travis looks at me for a moment and I know. I know he's going to bring it up and tell the doctor I'm a nut case.

"I've asked Derek, but until he sends me the info I need, what should I know about Borderline Personality Disorder?" The doctor looks shocked for a split second before realization dawns on him.

"Ah, I get it now." I glare at them both, super ready to tell them to get fucked and where to go, and if Circuit wasn't being held prisoner at the cabin, I totally would. But I need him.

Fuck it all to hell.

"Get what?" Travis asks him, looking confused as hell.

"If you're referring to Rina having BPD..." He looks at me and I sigh, nodding. "Then she's having an episode right now. That's where some of her attitude came from." Just some? Pfft, maybe the doc is a cracker barrel. That's where it all came from, but I won't tell him that.

"Some?"

Doctor Evans nods. "I wouldn't say everything today was her BPD, but it was probably about eighty-five percent her episode. Individuals with Borderline Personality Disorder have a hard time regulating their emotions. They often can have manic or depressive episodes, but not fully in the way a bi-polar person would." Travis nods along and I'm just sitting here steaming mad. Wait.

"Who the hell is Derek?!" I snap, cutting them off.

"That was maybe half her BPD talking and half sass, just FYI," the doctor points out, and I literally want to kill him right now.

"Go to hell. You don't know me from Eve. I have

every right to be snappy right now!" I holler, and he gives me a small nod before the good sheriff speaks.

"Derek is my little brother. He's a psychiatrist in Kansas." He shrugs before turning back to the doctor. "How can I tell if it's her BPD or if it's just her being mouthy?"

Doctor Evans is quiet for a moment, thinking it over.

How dare he? How dare they?! I am not mouthy!

"I assume she's given you some trouble since you met?" Travis nods and I growl, making him smirk. Asshole.

"You have no idea." Again, I repeat. Asshole!

"Was she making eye contact with you?" Travis sits back, thinking about my previous 'behaviour', and I scrunch up my nose as I remember as well.

Fuck it all to hell, he's right. When I was just being pissy, I stood toe to toe with the giant ogre without looking away, but this morning I haven't made eye contact at all.

"She was. At least, she was until this morning." His eyes connect with mine, and I shrink into myself. I really hate the attention on me.

"Rina?" Doctor Evans says my name and waits until I'm looking at him. "What triggered you?"

"Nothing." I refuse to tell them this bullshit going on in my head. No fucking way, batman.

"Pixie, you promised me you wouldn't lie to the doctor, did you not?" Travis asks, and I grumble under my breath.

Damn him and his locked memory. I can't exactly go back on a promise. "Yes."

"Good girl." God, why does that fill me with so much warmth? I'm a strong woman, I should not feel so much joy from a man praising me, but Travis is different.

I don't know how it's different, but it is. Maybe I'll even have time to figure it out.

"I tried to run away last night and then I got emotional." They stay silent, waiting for me to continue. "When I get overwhelmed, I have this backfire in my brain and it makes me mental and fucked up."

They're both looking at me like I've lost the plot and I can't blame them.

"What do you mean your brain backfires? What happens? Can you explain it to me?"

Oh God, do I actually have to say it?

Yes, because you promised the sheriff you would be honest.

Oh, shut it, inner monologue.

I take a few deep breaths, looking at the ground and sigh.

"I act like a little kid, alright?! I'm a freak and the sheriff witnessed my inner psycho." Neither of them makes a sound so I look up to see the disgust on their faces, but it's not there. Instead, all I see is pity and I think I hate that even more.

Sure, pity the mental head case.

"Did you know age regression is one hundred percent a coping mechanism for people with traumatic pasts?" That's what Doctor Evans says instead. "And a lot of people actually enjoy it."

"Hate to disappoint, doc, but I've been this way my entire life." He shares a look with Travis, who moves to squat in front of me.

"That's okay too, Pixie girl." How can they be so nice to me after all of this? How can they not see that I'm a completely fucked up freak? "Did you enjoy being Little last night?"

Being little? What is he talking about?

"I don't get why you're calling it that." I look between him and the doc and then focus back on him.

"I think you're a natural born Little. I know you don't really understand what that means, and I can explain it more back at home if you don't want

Richard listening, but I think you enjoyed feeling Little last night until the self-hate took over."

"You've already seen it?" Doc asks and Travis nods, not looking away from me.

"A couple times in the past few days, but it's almost instantly followed by her clamming up and shutting me out."

"That would be the BPD part of her brain. Most BPD sufferers struggle with self-acceptance and self-love in any form. If she thinks it's something to be ashamed of, she will close herself off."

"Okay, you guys need to tell me what you're talking about because I'm lost."

"Have you heard of BDSM?" Travis asks, holding my hands in his. I narrow my eyes.

"What does rough and kinky sex have to do with any of this?" I swear to God he groans, adjusting himself on his feet before looking back at me.

"There's another side to BDSM. A softer side for Littles and Middles." There's that word *little* again.

Wait...

"Is that why you call me little girl all the time?"

He smiles and shrugs. "Partly. You're also just really tiny, Pix."

I give up. "So, BDSM Littles and Middles? You're

going to have to give me more than that if you want me to follow along here."

"Right. Sorry." He clears his throat. "I'm what you call a Daddy Dom. I feel the need to nurture and care for Littles and Middles, though I'm more drawn to Littles such as yourself." He winks and holy Hannah, someone help my poor heart. "Some Littles and Middles choose age regression as a form of therapy like Richard said. It takes them out of their adult space and helps them relax and de-stress. To cope when things get hard."

I shake my head. "I already told you, I don't do that. This isn't a choice for me. I'm just fucked up."

He growls, grabbing my chin in one hand. "There is nothing wrong with you, Rina. The next time you put yourself down, I'm going to tan your hide after washing your mouth out with soap." He then turns to Doc. "Can I punish her when she has BPD?"

Doc nods. "I don't see why not. But if she's in an episode, you will have to wait until she's out of it before you act on it. Discuss everything with her first and make sure she understands what behaviours she is and is not being punished for. There are a lot of things about BPD that she has no control over, including her anger."

The sheriff nods, taking it all in and I feel pissed. I've decided that he's *the sheriff* when I'm mad at him.

"Hello, I'm right here and I have not given you permission to punish me. And for the record, I never will."

He shrugs and gives me a smirk. "We'll see. Now, where were we? Right. Some Littles and Middles are just born that way. It doesn't make them weird or messed up like you seem to think you are. It just means they need that mental break from adulting or thinking for themselves."

This all sounds stupid if you ask me.

They didn't, and don't even try to pretend what he's saying doesn't interest you.

God, will you shut up?!

Technically, I'm you so... no. Because you would have to shut up and we both know that's not something you do well.

Ugh, I hate my brain.

"Are you making this up?" I look between him and the doc as they both shake their heads.

Well, fuck.

"So, you think I'm a Little?" Travis nods. "And you think, what? That I should give into the inner psycho? Hey, don't look at me like that. It's just what

I've always called her and she's really mouthy, by the way."

He snorts. "Oh, Pixie. I'm very well acquainted with her. She's been around a lot more than you realize the past couple days." Shit, shit, shit. How did that happen without me noticing?

"Speaking as your doctor, I absolutely think you should try this as homework."

I groan. "You clearly didn't know me in school, Doc, but homework is bad news bears."

He chuckles, looking at Travis. "She's a sassy one, isn't she?" He sounds amused before looking back at me. "I don't want you to push yourself or do anything you're uncomfortable with, but can you promise me something?"

I sigh, nodding. Damn the men in this town and their freaking promises! "Yeah, sure. Why not? Can't be worse than you sticking me with a bunch of needles."

Travis shakes his head like I'm being dramatic, but it wasn't him that got stabbed with the little pricky thing. I'm convinced doctors are just new age vampires and get blood this way instead of ripping a person's neck to pieces.

I mean, can those machines *really* read our blood? Think about it.

"The next time you're feeling yourself going Little, can you try to talk it out with Travis? He will know what to do and say to help her. She's safe with him."

Yeah, that's debatable. It's not so easy to just shut down the self-loathing that's programmed into my mind.

"I'll try." They both nod before we say our good-byes and walk out of the office.

I guess as a doctor, he wasn't so bad after all.

CHAPTER 8
TRAVIS

OUT OF ALL THE THINGS THAT COULD HAVE HAPPENED today, I didn't expect to be sitting in my living room at the end of the night watching Rina devour books on the kindle Lana gave her.

I tried to get them to tell me what was on it, but there was no way to get them to say a word. They just giggled and trotted off like I hadn't just asked them a damn question.

My deputy sure has his hands full with that little one, the lucky bastard.

Not that I'm too far off. With every second that goes by, I find myself more drawn into Rina's spell and I hate knowing what she's been through the past couple months, but she had fun today.

I wasn't sure how a city girl like her would react

to the horses, but I figured this morning was going to be stressful for her after her slight freak out in the truck yesterday. I wanted to counter that with some peace and tranquility and another friendly face.

I don't know what it is about her that has my head spinning in circles, but I can't seem to stop it. Any of it.

Even my dick has taken notice of just how sexy and adorable she is, and the sass! That has my dick perkier than he's been in years, the fucking traitor. But I can't make a move on her. She needs to finally feel safe and at peace somewhere and I will cut my own arm off just to make sure I give that to her.

I will make it my mission to conquer her demons so she can choose for herself what she wants.

If the way I catch her looking at me from time to time is any indication, I know she's interested in me too, but one thing at a time.

"Holy damn," I hear her whisper and it pulls me out of my thoughts. Her face is flushed and she's breathing heavily. What the hell is she reading?

"What are you doing, Pixie girl?" Her head flies up, looking at me with wide eyes, and I smirk. *Yeah, baby, I caught you being turned on. Now what are you going to do about it?*

"Have you heard of cock warming?"

What the...huh? "Excuse me?" She gives me an amused look. "First off, what the hell is cock warming? Do I want to know? Also, what the fuck are you reading? I don't think little girls should be reading about whatever...this...is!" I feel exasperated as she giggles on the couch, holding the kindle to her stomach.

"It's in this book. It's my first Daddy book and it's actually super cool, and oof." She fans herself and I feel my dick rising. Dear Lord, please save me from myself.

Wait...

"You're reading a Daddy book?" She smiles and nods, looking mighty pleased with herself. "And?"

She shrugs. "I think I'm a lot like Juliet. I mean, I totally feel her pain from having a fucked up past, you know? Mine isn't nearly as devastating as hers, but I like it."

Grant me patience.

"Oookay? Who is Juliet?" I have no idea what I'm about to get myself into, but I want to keep hearing her voice.

"Oh! She's this super sweet and quiet Little in this book by Laylah Roberts. I think she may end up being my favourite author if this book is any indication of her writing! I can't wait to read about more hot cowboys!" she practically squeals, and I have to remind myself it's just a fucking book. But if she wants a cowboy Daddy, I'm more than happy to oblige.

"Right. Okay, so where does cock warming come into play? And what is it?"

"You mean it's not a normal Daddy/Little thing?"

"I don't know, Pixie. You'd have to explain it to me first."

She frowns. "But if it was a normal part of this, wouldn't you already know?"

"Please just tell me what it is?" Maybe being gentle will get her to stop beating around the bush. I'm not sure my sanity and dick can take it.

"Okay, well in this book—it's called *Her Daddies Saving Grace* by the way—she has two Daddies."

"Nope. Not happening, little girl. You want me, you have me. I'm enough."

She actually pouts at me. "But, but what if I need two Daddies to be happy? I mean, I'm a lot for poor old you to handle."

Deep breaths man. Deep fucking breaths. In and out. "Do you need two Daddies?"

She shrugs. "That remains to be seen. I'm super new to this. You sure you'd be up for the task?" That's when I see it. That glint of mischief in her eye and I know I'm fucked. I will go to the ends of the earth and back for this girl and it hasn't even been forty-eight hours.

I'm screwed.

"If you find out that it's something you need, we can discuss it then." Her eyes widen in shock before narrowing.

"You'd share me?!" she screeches and I groan. Are there seriously any right answers here?

"Not fucking likely, but we're getting off topic. What is cock warming?"

"Oh, right. Sorry, my bad. I mean, technically I'm not even yours." She shrugs but I catch the look of sadness in her eyes before she continues. "One of her Daddies uses it as an anxiety trick. When she's really upset or anxious, she takes his penis into her mouth and gently sucks on it like a soother."

Nope. My dick can't take it.

I'm officially hard as a fucking rock the second she quits talking because I imagine a doe-eyed Rina kneeling in front of me, sucking on my dick.

Coughing, I adjust myself on the chair to try and ease the pressure that this apparently not so innocent conversation has caused.

How do I get myself into these kinds of situations? *Right, because these kinds of things happen so often. Dumbass.*

"Uhm, no it's not a normal Daddy/little thing. I think it's an individual thing and I haven't actually heard it used quite like that before." Not that the idea doesn't have merit for the right Little. "Is that... something you think you'd like?"

She scrunches her nose at me. "Nah, if I have a cock in my mouth, I want that bitch going down my throat and choking me."

Ah fuck.

"Right. New rule, Pix. No swearing unless you're scared, in danger, or being thoroughly fucked to within an inch of your life."

Her mouth opens and closes before she puts the kindle down and glares at me. "Oh, and you're the language police now?"

Not going there.

I choose a different tactic. I'm not stupid enough to take that head-on. No fucking way. Women are vicious and this girl definitely has claws. I bet she bites too.

"You're reading about Daddies and Littles, and you seem interested. Is that something you'd like to try out?" She goes from annoyed to concentrating, and I mentally pat myself on the back for deflecting that conversation.

"I think I'd like to. It sounds like something I could benefit from, and like you and Doc pointed out, I'm already a Little. Right?"

I nod. "You are."

"And you're a Daddy?"

I nod, smiling. "Yeah, baby, I am."

She looks at the device and then back at me and nods. "Yes. I would really like to try it, but I can't promise anything. I have a mouth on me."

I chuckle. "Oh, sweet Pixie girl, I know and I will come up with consequences for them."

She sucks in a breath. "Like what?"

"Like soap for swearing or mouthing off for no good reason."

"Grooooss!" She gags and I shrug.

"Actions have consequences, baby."

She shivers and bites her lip. "Would...would this have to be sexual?"

I stop short. "No, not at all. If being with me is something you don't want, then we can do this platonically." Not that I've seen it done personally. I know it's done though.

"And if I did want there to be... you know?" She's

blushing and I can't help but puff out my chest like a moron.

"Then we take this one step at a time. Your life is still in danger, and this is all very new to you. But I won't take you until you know this is without a doubt something that you want, because I need to be a Daddy, and I won't toy with you."

She looks like she's about to cry and I curse myself for possibly saying something to upset her. "You'd really want me?"

I blink, not expecting her to ask me that. Does she not know her self-worth?

Then I remember reading over some of the stuff on BPD that Derek sent me while the girls were playing around at Serenity. People with BPD have a tendency to think the worst of themselves and others and constantly believe they aren't good enough.

"Definitely. You're beautiful, strong, sassy as all hell, and you're smart. And let's not forget brave." I stand up and move over to sit beside her on the couch.

"I don't believe all that," she admits shyly, and I nod.

"That's okay. I will help you believe it in time, but just know that I believe it, so it has to be true. Know why?" She looks at me, tears brimming in her eyes and shakes her head. "Because I'm never wrong." She snorts then falls over laughing so hard I feel like I may need to do CPR to help her breathe again.

At least it got the laugh I was hoping for, and the only trace of tears are from laughter.

"Old man, you got yourself a deal. I guess now the question is...where do we start?"

Oh, I have a whole lot of ideas on where we can start and none of them are appropriate at this point. My dick needs to shut the fuck up.

"Tonight,, my beautiful Pixie girl, we get some sleep. We can talk about everything else in the morning."

She actually pouts at me, and I feel something in my chest warming.

"Ugh, fine. Whatever, old man. Wouldn't want to keep you up past your bedtime."

I swear to fuck her sass is going to end me.

CHAPTER 9
RINA

RULES.

So many fucking rules it actually hurts my head to think about it. Like how am I seriously supposed to follow them all? I swear he's setting me up for punishments on purpose.

Fine. I might be slightly over dramatic, but geez, this is gonna take some getting used to.

"Is this really necessary?" I whine, and he just blinks at me.

"You're not a morning person and you get excessively cranky when you don't sleep."

I grumble. "I've only been here a couple days. Did you think about that?" He tilts his head to the side like he's assessing my reasons.

"Can you truthfully tell me you're not normally like this?" He raises an eyebrow in question.

"No," I mumble.

He nods. Bedtimes are such a shitty idea.

"Didn't think so, Pixie. Besides, from everything my brother has sent me about BPD, I know that a proper sleep routine will benefit you and your emotions while helping to regulate your moods." Damn him and his logical reasoning. It would be easier to lie to him if he wasn't coming at this from a place of genuine concern.

"I know you're right."

He gives me a small smile, taking my hand in one of his. "I know this will take some getting used to, but I think it's going to be great for you." I think he's right, but I still can't shake that something is just going to upend my happiness and my life. It's not like I can hide from Robert forever.

He will find me.

"Whatever that thought was, I don't like it." He lets out a small growl and I jump slightly.

"Huh?" He softens, pulling me into his lap and dear Lord, this is where I would like to spend the rest of my days. Please and thank you!

"You were annoyed with the rules, like any Little would be, but then your face went from annoyance to sadness and fear." I sigh, picking at the t-shirt against his chest. The man is definitely solid. "You know a huge part of this dynamic is honesty, right, Rina?"

I sniffle and nod. "I know. I just need a little more time, please?" He kisses my head, laying me deeper against his chest and sighs.

"I don't need exact specifics right this second, but I need to know something, baby. I need to know what all I can do to keep you safe." I wish he could.

I wish I hadn't brought this crap to their town, and I really wish I could walk away from Travis and everything, but I'm too tired.

I'm tired of running and being afraid. I'm tired of not living a normal damn life.

"My father wants to kill me." I sigh as he stiffens.

"Your Dad is the one who wants your inheritance?"

I nod. "Yeah. He's never been an overly nice person to me, and he never wanted a kid. Anyway, he has a gambling problem and lost all his inheritance. My grandparents didn't trust him, so they made it impossible for him to even be a guardian over the trust they left for me," I whisper.

"And he's so hard up for money he would kill his only child?" He's not certain I'm an only child, but it's a fair guess and he'd be right. It would have been a lot harder to run if I had a sibling to watch over and protect as well.

"Yeah, pretty much." I shrug, pulling back to look at him. "They never imagined they wouldn't still be here when I was twenty-five, and I honestly don't think they figured their son would stoop so low as to kill his own kid. Even if he was abusive."

"Shit." He lets out a harsh breath and moves me around until I'm straddling his thighs, facing him, but it's not sexual. There is only pain and sadness in those eyes, and it's all for me. "I'm sorry your father is such a bastard, Pixie girl." He cups my cheek and I lean into the warmth of his hand, closing my eyes.

I just want to stay like this. This is the most at peace I've felt since I was a little girl.

"When Grandma died a few months back, I started noticing things." He watches me, waiting for me to continue. "At first, I thought it was my anxiety and paranoia because of the way my brain works, but after a while... I knew I was being followed." Darkness envelopes his eyes to a scary degree and his grip on my cheek tightens slightly.

"Did you go to the police?" I shake my head, not wanting to look at him, but I don't have to. "They're crooked, aren't they? That's why you hated me on sight. Why you have a hard time trusting anyone?"

God, can this man get anymore perfect?

"Yes," I whisper, feeling myself shaking, and he pulls my forehead to his.

"I will never hurt you, Rina. I know you have trust issues, and this will take time, but I promise you that you can trust me and my team." I swallow and nod, my nose rubbing against his.

"I know. It's going to sound insane or crazy, but I trust you more than I trust anyone. No one has ever taken the time to learn about my illness or even to see past my attitude to wonder what may be under it."

"They're all idiots, baby."

I snort and he chuckles softly, his soft breath tingling my lips. "Some would say that about you for taking on a whack job like me."

He growls, his hand moving into my hair and pulling hard.

"That will be the last time I let you put yourself down, Rina. Next time, there will be consequences." See? Rules. But how am I supposed to just stop myself from being negative after doing it for years? "Tell me the rules we went over, Pixie." I sigh and groan, pulling back to pout and he shakes his head, smiling. "Please?"

"Using your insane hotness is totally not fair," I point out before continuing. "Don't ever go anywhere alone. My health and safety are always first and foremost to you." He nods, giving my hips a gentle squeeze. "Tell you everything as I feel it, but don't hide anything from you. If I see anything out of the ordinary, I'm to tell you instantly whether my brain makes me feel like I'm crazy or not."

"Good girl. Keep going." I relax into his praise. I don't know why it feels so good to have someone give it to me, but it's nice.

"Bedtime is at ten." I scrunch my nose and he chuckles.

"I could make you take daily naps."

I gasp. "No!"

He smiles and shrugs. "I may do it anyway from time to time."

I groan but keep going.

"My safeword for anything and everything we are doing is red to stop, and yellow to slow down, but if I'm scared or feel danger, or something is off, I just have to ask for Starbursts." I hate them because they get stuck in my teeth. The consistency is just wrong in my opinion, so it was something we both knew I would never ask for.

Travis is kind of a genius, and it's a little scary knowing how much of this stuff he is prepped for.

"I'm proud of you for remembering all of that and for taking a chance on this. For going out of your comfort zone and trusting me enough to help you find yourself and be happy." I beam.

"I like when you do that."

"Do what?" he asks confused and I smile.

"Compliment me."

He nods. "You deserve it and so much more, Rina. I will help you see that eventually."

"Thank you." I lean in and kiss him gently on the lips before pulling back to see his reaction.

He watches me, waiting to see if I'm going to run scared or not. He must realize I'm not because he cups my cheek and pulls me back down for a soft and languid kiss that has me feeling like a puddle of goo.

We kiss for a moment like that, neither of us trying to take it deeper before he pulls me back a little and I whine.

"Slow. Let's build trust and communication first, okay?" I nod and move off his lap before he sighs.

"You ready to join me at work today?" he asks in a teasing voice, and I groan.

"Nope, but at least I have all these books to read." I wink and skip off to change as he mumbles something about talking to Trent about the books Lana gave me.

Travis

If looks could kill, I'm not sure who would be dead right now. Sammi or myself, but fuck, does Rina look mad.

It's not my fault Sammi came into the station with a pizza I didn't ask for and I've been trying to quietly shut her flirting down, but she's not taking the hint and my girl is getting pissed off. I'm just not sure if it's because we agreed to a dynamic together and she's jealous because we agreed to take the physical things slow, outside of punishments. Or if she's got something against women like Sammi because of her past.

I know nothing about her mother aside from the woman up and ditching her child with an abusive asshole, so maybe it's that? Though logically, I know jealousy when I see it. I need to shut this down before she gets sassy and starts something.

"Sammi," I say, holding up my hand to get her to stop. Please don't let this come out wrong.

"Yes, Sheriff?" She's practically purring at me and I know Rina heard her. My poor Pixie girl is vibrating in the chair outside my office.

"I appreciate you bringing me my favourite pizza." She blushes, smiling widely at me and I internally groan. Fuck, I'm about to crush her, aren't I? "You're a very sweet woman, Sammi, but I'm afraid the flirting has to stop."

She blinks at me, looking confused. "You don't like me?" Why is that always the first thing women jump to? I mean, I don't like her in that way, but still. Women need to stop that shit.

"It's not that I don't like you as a person, but I'm really not interested in you that way. I should have said something sooner, but I didn't want to hurt you."

She lets out a little huff or whine. "Why now? Flirting is harmless." She pouts and I can see my

Pixie sitting up straighter in the chair and glaring at Sammi's back.

"It might be if we were both available, but I'm not."

She scrunches up her nose. "But I know for a fact that you're single, Travis."

Rina's eyes narrow at me, waiting for my reply and I groan, pinning her with a quick look that says 'don't' and I hope she listens.

"I'm not, actually."

Sammi grunts, her head turning towards my girl who quickly turns away from us again, before Sammi turns back to me. "Her? She's a little wrong for you, Sheriff, don't you think?"

Wrong thing to say.

Rina jumps up and comes barreling into the office. I swear steam would be coming out of her ears if she were a cartoon character.

Getting up, I quickly grab her and hold her against my chest to stop her from doing something stupid. Not that I won't stick up for her, but I know she doesn't get that yet.

"Sammi, I know you know that was rude." I watch her as she seems to realize her mistake and looks at the ground.

"I'm sorry, Sheriff. I wasn't meaning to be rude, I

just always figured you would give me a chance eventually." I squeeze Rina tighter against me to stop her from saying anything.

Sammi is a submissive too. I'm not sure if she's a Little or not, but I don't want her feelings being torn down either.

"I'm sorry if I gave you that hope, but I'm happy with Rina. It's new, but she's everything I didn't even know I wanted or needed. You will find happiness, Sammi. It just won't be with me."

She nods, sniffing before she looks at us. "Okay, thank you, Sheriff. And for what it's worth, I'm sorry if I upset you, Rina."

Rina gives her a curt nod before leaning back into me and I don't try to force her to speak. I know this is probably a lot for her already and she may be feeling emotionally overwhelmed. I would never make her do something when I'm not sure where her head is at.

Once Sammi is gone, I let go of Rina and move over to close the office door before pulling her to the small couch in the corner.

"You alright, Pixie girl?"

She groans and lays her head on my shoulder. "Truthfully?"

I nod. "Always, Rina."

She lets out a breath and shakes her head. "No. I'm annoyed and angry at her, but more than anything, I'm scared."

When we had our talk this morning about going through with this dynamic, making the rules, etc., one of them was that she would always be honest with me and if she couldn't, she would say I can't right now.

I'm extremely proud of her for communicating with me, but now I need to know what's causing the fear because it's something I hadn't expected.

"Annoyed and angry I get, but why fear? What are you afraid of?"

"Promise to not think I'm stupid?" Fuck, it kills me that she even has to ask that. There is no world in which I would think she was stupid or dumb so I tell her that and it seems to calm her a little. "Okay. I'm afraid that she's right. I mean, I doubt I'm the normal type of girl you go for, and that's not even including the fact that you arrested me or that I have a lot of secrets."

"Secrets that you promised to share with me as you're ready." She nods, lifting her head to look at me.

"If I tell you a secret, do you promise to not look me up? Trust me that running my name will tell them where I am? Though they've probably figured it out already." She swallows, looking pale and afraid and I want to kill them.

"I promise I won't run your name through the system, Pixie. And as far as anyone coming into this town, Trent and I are keeping our eyes open for any newcomers. I won't let anything happen to you."

She gets this look of sadness on her face. "I know you believe that, but what if he hurts you? He won't stop until he's killed me, Travis."

"I just found you, Rina, and I'm sure as hell not going to let you go. It's one of the reasons you can't go anywhere alone right now. If I'm with you, then you're protected. I won't let anyone get close enough to hurt you." There are so many things I wish I could make her believe, but she's been living her entire life in fear of her father in one sense or another, so a couple days isn't going to just magically make her feel secure.

"You make me feel happier than anything I've had in a long time. Even if something were to happen to me, I'm glad I met you and get to call you mine. Even if it is just for a little while," she whispers, and I can't take it anymore.

"Baby, I'm hoping it's more than just a little while. I'm kind of hoping it's forever." She sucks in a breath, her eyes searching my face and she starts to cry a little.

God, it hurts to watch her cry. "You're kind of an amazing Daddy, you know that?" She throws her arms around my neck, and I catch her easily, my arms wrapping around her while I try and wrap my head around what she said.

"Pixie? Did you just call me Daddy?" I rasp and she nods into my neck, sniffing and squeezing her arms tighter, and I sigh into her. I thought it would take a lot longer for her to call me Daddy than it did, but fuck, do I love it.

"Uh huh."

"God, baby. You have no idea how incredible it is to hear that." I swallow the emotions in my throat. "I've never really been called Daddy before."

She pulls back looking sad and confused. "What do you mean?"

I move my arms to rest at her lower back. "Well, I've never had my own Little before. Never found someone who I could call my own. I've had girlfriends, even serious ones, but none of them filled the need of being a Daddy Dom. Even at the club, I didn't let the Subs and Littles I played with call me Daddy because I wasn't their Dom. It was always Sir or Master."

She blinks at me. "There's a club you go to?" She lifts an eyebrow, and I'm not sure if she's curious or worried.

"Yep. It's a BDSM club a buddy of mine owns. I haven't been there in a while, though. It just wasn't fulfilling me like I wanted it to."

More adorable blinking. "Huh."

I snort, not even sure how to interpret that. "Say what you want to say, but do it respectfully, so you don't wind up with a hot bottom." She pouts and whines at me. God, she's cute.

"If I don't want to ever go into a place like that, would you be upset?" I watch her face, trying to read between the lines because I know it can't be as simple as that, but I reassure her anyways.

"Not at all. We already discussed I'm not into hardcore BDSM. Anything we want to do, we can easily do it at home and I wouldn't care. But that's not all you're asking, is it?" She shakes her head, looking down between us. "Are you worried I would try to do a scene with someone else?" She nods, still not looking at me and I won't have it.

Lifting her chin with my finger, I look deep into her misty eyes. "Sweet Pixie girl, I would never cheat on you, and if you don't want to go to *Ignition,* then I'm fine with that."

"Really?" She gives me a small smile and I move my face closer to hers.

"Really, really." She giggles and I pull her to me, our mouths meeting, and I have to hold in the groan trying to escape.

Her lips are soft as hell, and I barely felt them this morning. I didn't want to push her past what she may be ready for, but this is different. She's called me Daddy and she knows I want to keep her forever.

I need to kiss her.

Moving my hands to cup her ass with one hand and her face with the other, I run my tongue along the seam of her lips until she whimpers, letting me in.

Her tongue tentatively glides against mine and I groan into her mouth, gripping her ass tighter, making her body jerk forward. Fuck, she feels incredible.

I let our tongues explore, our moans muffled by the other as the kiss continues until I have to pull back. If I keep kissing her like this, we will start something I refuse to finish in my office. I also know that, as much as we both want to take this further, we need to pace ourselves. I told her I wouldn't be intimate with her until I had fully gained her trust and we just aren't there yet.

"Wow." Her breathing is ragged, and I smirk, making her scowl.

"Yeah, wow. Now, what do you say we go home and watch a movie before bed?" She looks thoughtful for a moment before blushing and turning shy. "Unless you have another idea?"

She bites her bottom lip and nods. If she were to look down between us right now, she'd see the tent I'm sporting in my jeans and that could be awkward.

"I kind of want to... umm play?" My dick jerks and she looks down between us, blushing even more. Fuck, she's sweet.

She doesn't mean sexually, idiot. Chill out.

If only the bastard would listen. He hasn't been this interested in someone in a long ass time.

"We can do whatever you want, Pixie girl." She beams at me, looking back down at my dick and I have to close my eyes to try and get some control over myself.

"K, but um... I don't have any money." I open my eyes to see her frowning.

"What do you need money for?"

"I want to play with Play-Doh."

I smile at her. "It just so happens that Daddy has a recipe for homemade Play-Doh, but for tonight I think we should just stop at the store and pick some up." I wink at her, and I can tell she wants to argue. "No arguing with Daddy. He's allowed to spoil his girl if he wants to. It's a rule."

She rolls her eyes at me, and I swat her ass playfully. "You and your rules are going to be the death of me, Daddy."

Snorting, I help her up before we start gathering our things to go home.

"I highly doubt that, Pix." She rolls her eyes again before growing serious. "What is it?"

She takes a deep breath. "My real name is Katrina Flemming."

My heart rate picks up as I realize how much courage and trust that took.

"I love it. It's very... you. Almost as beautiful as Pixie." I wink at her, and she giggles, the stress once again leaving her shoulders. "Thank you for trusting me, Rina. I won't let you down, I promise." She smiles at me, her brown eyes bright and beautiful.

"I know."

CHAPTER 10
RINA

TOTALLY ONE HUNDRED PERCENT WHAT I NEEDED.

Did you know they make glitter Play-Doh?! Because I sure as heck didn't and Daddy totally went overboard on buying it for me when I squealed.

I should be embarrassed how excited I got, but seriously? It's freaking GLITTER PLAY-DOH!!!! I legit can't even be mad.

Being Little is actually kind of amazing. I don't feel nearly as upset or anxious as I usually do about Robert trying to kill me, and I'm smiling. Like who the heck am I right now?

"What are you building, Pixie girl?" Daddy asks me when he comes back into the room, and I sigh contently. He does that. Keeps leaving the room to give me space in case I get too tense since this is so new but keeps checking on me to remind me I'm not alone.

I get why he's doing it, but it kind of totally sucks donkey balls.

"What do you think it is, Daddy?" I beam up at him and he looks at my creations like he's deep in thought.

I totally get that it's legit just blobs of stuff looking like nothing, but in my Little mindset right now, it's a towering underwater castle for the princess mermaid.

That's what they call the pretty stuff. Mermaid Play-Doh. Genius, right?

"Hmm, is it Daddy's station?" I snort in a less than ladylike fashion and start giggling at the look he gives me. "Did you just snort like a pig at Daddy?" He lifts an eyebrow, and I can tell he's trying hard not to smile right now.

"Well, duh. Why would I want to use such pretty things to build a boring sheriff's station?" I roll my eyes and he narrows his.

"I will have you know, little girl, that my station is anything but boring."

"Sure, Daddy. Keep telling yourself that, but it's super boring. I slept there, remember? It's cold and blah, and the bed smells icky."

He grimaces. "Sorry, baby. Drunk Dave had been in there the night before. Usually, it has time to air out before someone is stuck in there after him."

"You know, I wouldn't have been in there if you hadn't been such a big ol' ogre meanie pants," I huff, and he shakes his head like he's being very serious.

"And what should I have done with the little girl who was breaking all kinds of rules that night? She definitely couldn't have been let go. That goes against all kinds of rules." He nods his head like he makes perfect sense, and I can't stop the belly laughter.

"I'm pretty sure you threw the rule book out on this one, Daddy. Is it normal to bring them home and claim them for your own like a pirate claiming his treasure?" His eyes sparkle and I freeze.

Uh-oh. That looks like I'm about to get it.

"You know, I haven't really claimed you yet, baby."

I snort and sober up before narrowing my eyes at him. "Then what do you call what you did to that poor kid in the store? You practically pissed a circle around me. And you growled at him!"

Another growl leaves his throat as he grabs my hand and pulls me up and into his arms.

"He was staring at your ass, baby. You agreed to

be mine, so I was just making sure he kept to himself. It is completely disrespectful for any man to stare at a woman like she's a piece of ass."

I roll my eyes because, seriously! He was just being helpful. "You were a caveman, Travis."

"Your caveman." I shrug, a feeling of sadness washing over me. "Hey, what was that about? What just happened, Pixie?" He looks so concerned, I don't even know how to explain my wayward thoughts to him.

Like, I know he says he wants this forever, which is totally weird since we just met, right? And if I wasn't so sure my life would be ending soon, I would feel the same way. I do feel the same way, just my forever is going to be a lot shorter than his. He will go on to someone else like that horrible pizza lady, Sammi, who would not stop flirting with him. UGH!

"Now that look was jealousy." He's smug as shit while he holds me tighter against his chest, his hands running up and down my spine and I sigh.

"I'm scared."

He sighs. "I know you are, Rina. It's okay to be scared. Your father seems like one hell of a piece of work."

I pull back, glaring at him. "You promised you

wouldn't look him up! He's going to find me here!" I shriek, my heart racing in my chest.

"I didn't use my system, sweetheart. I called a friend of mine at the FBI. He owed me a favour, so he ran a background check and sent it to me in a secure email." I deflate a little, but I'm still on edge.

Fuck, what if they track that email back to Travis? What if he gets hurt because of me?

"You shouldn't have done that! He could come after you now, too!" I feel myself slipping from reality and into my head, his words sounding more and more muffled.

"Baby, you need to calm down and breathe before you pass out." I can't. I can't think or hear him. I barely feel myself moving as he takes us over to the couch before sitting down on it.

Well, he is. I'm perched in his lap which I would normally be pleased about, but I'm panicking and numb.

This can't be happening.

"Baby, I need you to hear me. You're freaking me out a little right now."

I hear a snort above us, and I can see myself kind of floating around like I'm not really in my own body anymore.

"You're totally freaking him out right now."

I sigh to myself, or my other self, I guess? God, I swear people would think I'm insane right now. Travis probably does too.

Why does this have to be who I am? Why can't I just be freaking normal? Sometimes I swear I'm some sort of science experiment gone wrong.

"You're not a science experiment, dumbass. You've suffered trauma. We've suffered trauma. This is just our brain's way of coping with a reality that's too hard to handle sometimes."

I nod to myself like I'm actually having a conversation with another version of me.

I know it's fucking weird, but it's like I have no control over my body. I can see myself losing all control and I'm trying to talk myself down, but my body doesn't want to listen.

You know how in some movies and tv shows, the soul is hanging over their body while they are on life support or having surgery and they try to lay back into their own body, but it doesn't work?

That's totally what it feels like when I have a meltdown or BPD episode that sends me into panic mode. Sometimes I can catch it in time, but sometimes it happens so damn fast, it's like I just got off some sort of spinning ride and I can't catch my bearings.

Fuck, I know I sound insane, but it's the best way I can explain it to people.

"Stop caring what other people think. Stop caring what you think, too! Just focus on the man trying to bring you back to him. Breathe, Rina, and focus on him. He will help bring you back, you know he will. Just focus and breathe."

I remind myself over and over again that I am in control of myself, and I can do this. That I've conquered this shit before, and I will do it again because I am a motherfucking badass warrior, and nothing will stop me.

"Hey, baby. I've got you." Travis' voice starts to sound closer the more I repeat my mantra and focus on my breathing until I'm fully back in the here and now. "There she is. Are you okay?" He watches me worriedly when my eyes meet his.

"I'm okay, Daddy." My voice is higher pitched than normal, but I'm not fighting it. I feel safer when I retreat into this space in my head. Even before I knew about Littles, I would retreat into what I called my mental breakdowns because it felt safer.

He must sense that I'm not adult me right now because he goes with it.

"My sweet Pixie girl. Can you tell Daddy what

happened?" I shake my head, pushing my thumb into my mouth, and he gently pulls me closer.

"Shhh, it's okay. Do you want to be Little Rina for the rest of the night?" I nod into his neck, and he blows out a breath. "Okay, we can do that, baby. Do you want Daddy to take over?" I nod again, closing my eyes, sucking on my thumb and completely content to just let him take over everything so I can just be.

Travis

My poor girl.

She's acting younger than I think I have ever seen her. I'm not sure I even thought she could go this little and I'm wondering if she even knew.

The only time I saw her suck her thumb was when she was asleep at the station that first night. Maybe she retreated into herself because she was so scared, and this may be her way of protecting herself?

I reach to pull out my phone to send Derek a message, but her whimpers stop me.

"Shh, I've got you, Pixie. I've got you." I can

always message him later. Right now, she needs to be my sole focus.

I'm not going to lie and say she didn't freak me out a few minutes ago. I tried to get her attention, but she just stared off into space like she couldn't hear a word I was saying.

She was nodding her head and mumbling things under her breath, but I couldn't understand any of it. All I could do was sit there and keep talking to her as I hoped and prayed she came back to me.

I know I read that sometimes people with Borderline Personality Disorder will retreat into their minds to shield themselves, or separate themselves from the situation, so that may have been what she was doing.

When she finally did come back to me, her eyes were so sad before she called me Daddy and started sucking on her thumb. When she didn't verbally answer me after that, I had a feeling she was just too little to talk.

Is it bad that I'm thankful she was here with me and not someone else? I can handle any age of Little she needs to regress to in order to feel safe and okay, and I will always take care of her. But someone else might have taken advantage of her.

That shit I read on her father had me seething in

anger. He's one hell of a piece of work. No one deserves a parent like him in their life and her mother isn't much better. According to the intel, she ran away from his abusive ass when Rina was really young but chose to leave her behind.

God, I would love to wring both their necks for being shit parents, but at least her mother isn't trying to fucking kill her. I can't imagine any parent being able to kill their own child, especially over money, but I've been in this profession long enough to know a lot of bad shit happens every day. Doesn't mean I have to like it.

Soft snores pull me out of my thoughts. My Pixie's passed out on my chest, her thumb sitting in her mouth like the adorable girl she is.

Just looking at her so vulnerable and knowing she trusts me enough to be this way in front of me has my throat clogging with emotion.

Leaning my head against the back of the couch, I grab the throw blanket beside us and cover her up, just listening to the sounds of her quiet snoring.

CHAPTER 11
RINA

AFTER MY LAST BREAKDOWN, I CAN HONESTLY SAY I have had an amazing week.

Knowing that he saw me at my absolute worst and still wants to be around me and call me his Pixie girl, has been the best feeling I've ever had. Like I somehow finally found the place I belong in life, and it is everything I ever thought it would be and more.

Heck, I'm even behaving relatively well. Or at least well enough I haven't gotten one of his punishments yet. It's starting to make me wonder if he's worried about punishing me because of my BPD and I don't want that.

I want to be treated the way he thinks I need to be, not like some breakable glass object. So, I'm going to test him today. I need to know he's going to treat me without kid gloves so to speak.

"Pixie! You ready to go?"

"No," I curse under my breath.

Shit. I was trying to figure out ways to get punished and forgot about the time. I haven't even moved to change out of my jammies yet.

"Excuse me?" Travis walks to my bedroom door, and I scrunch up my nose.

Ooops.

"Um, no?" I repeat myself, but this time it comes out as more of a question and I want to mentally slap myself.

He crosses his arms over his chest and scans the bed I've been sleeping in. "Considering you're not dressed, I'm going to say that's pretty obvious," he replies drolly and I can feel the blush. "Question is, why aren't you dressed?"

"Umm..." I can't exactly come out with the truth, right? I mean, I'm not that stupid. He will think I've lost the plot if I tell him I was conjuring up ways to get punished. Now that I'm looking a possible punishment in the face, I'm beginning to question my own sanity.

What the heck was I thinking?

"Not an answer." His face takes on a concerned

look. "Are you okay? Has this week been too over-whelming for you?"

"NO! Fuck's sake man!" I snap, then throw my hand across my mouth as my eyes go wide.

Okay, so maybe I'm more sensitive to him treating me like glass than I thought, but can you freaking blame a girl? I know my sassy ass has been enough to at least get the so-called soap he keeps threatening me with. Not that I actually want it because...yuck.

"Right. That's it." He stalks toward me, and I yelp, trying to move back on the bed before he grabs my ankle. "I don't think so, little girl. You're going to tell me what is going on in that brain of yours right now." He pulls me to the edge of the bed, caging me in with his arms and getting right in my face.

Swallowing roughly, I do the one thing I can think of to get out of this.

"Nothing. Sorry, I don't think I slept well last night." The snort he lets out tells me he knows I'm full of shit. Crap on a cracker.

"Try again, Pixie. That's ten." I feel my eyes go wide.

"Ten what?" I squeak and he gives me an evil smile.

"Ten swats on that delicious bottom, and that's

not including the soap you're getting in your mouth before we leave this morning."

Oh, hell no!

"For what?!" I feel myself getting annoyed. "I didn't do anything!"

He narrows his eyes. "You lied to me, after swearing at me. Now, correct me if I'm wrong, but I distinctly remember one of your rules being that you have to be honest with Daddy and another being no swearing without good reason."

Well fudge fucker duck.

"Umm...I plead the fifth?" He snorts and shakes his head.

"This isn't a court of law, Pixie girl. Try again."

I huff out a breath. "What was the question?" Deflect and distract. That's the name of the game.

"Why you aren't dressed was the original question. But now I'm wondering why you snapped at Daddy a second ago?"

Should I tell him? Fuck it.

"Because I am sick and tired of you treating me with kid gloves, like I'm going to break!" His head rears back in shock, and I groan. That totally came out pissier than I thought it would.

"What are you talking about?"

I huff. "I know my mouth would have gotten me

into trouble by now. I've been swearing more than I should and I know I've mouthed back at you, but you haven't once tried to punish me." He looks confused.

"You're upset because I haven't punished you? It's only been a week, Pixie." He searches my face and I lift an eyebrow.

"If I had been any other Little or submissive, would you have let everything I've done or said slide?" I can see his mind working behind those beautiful green eyes before he sighs, hanging his head.

"No, I wouldn't have. But you're different, Pixie."

I growl. Legit growl at him and his lips twitch.

"I'm not! I don't need to be treated like glass, Travis. If I thought showing you the most vulnerable side of me was going to make you treat me differently, I never would have let you in," I snap and see the hurt across his face.

I want to cry for hurting him, but he has to realize that treating me differently is the exact opposite of what I want.

"I'm sorry," he whispers, clearing his throat before standing up. "I promise to do better, Rina. I don't want you to ever doubt me."

I nod, standing up and wrapping my arms around his waist. "I know, Daddy."

He sighs, kissing my head and hugging me tight. "Alright, into the bathroom you go. Let's get this over with."

"Get what over with?" I pretend to forget, and he raises his eyebrow like he's wondering if I really believe he forgot.

Ugh, so gross. I pout and stomp off to the bathroom with a slightly dramatic flair, but seriously! He's going to put soap in my mouth!

I watch as he follows me in and reaches under the sink to grab a fresh bar of soap. A really big one.

"Do you maybe have some of those little hotel soaps?"

He shakes his head at me. "So you can pull your tongue away from it without actually tasting the soap and learning your lesson? Not a chance." He wets the bar and suds it up a bit before holding it up. "Open."

Nope. No way.

"Da—" He pushes the soapy bar into my mouth. It lands solidly on my tongue, making me gag, but he holds it in there like he expected that reaction.

"Right. While you hold this on your tongue for a

minute, let's talk about *why* I don't like you swearing."

I mumble a couple choice words at him before gagging as the soap tries to escape down my throat.

"I'll pretend you didn't just try to swear at me again since that disgusted look on your face shows that you're actually learning something." I narrow my eyes but keep my mouth shut. Metaphorically speaking of course, since the giant grossness is keeping my mouth open.

"I don't like you swearing because I promise you, it's going to make it harder for you to go into little space. If you're fuming and stressed, little space is going to be a lot harder for you to reach and I don't want that for you." He takes a deep breath. "I want you to be able to easily access it whenever you need to retreat."

Aww, that's actually really sweet and my eyes start to water as he pulls the soap out.

"Spit and rinse your mouth out." I do, gagging a little as I fight to get the soap out of my mouth. When I'm finished, I turn back to him with my eyes downcast.

"I'm sorry. I didn't realize that was why." I sniffle and he sighs, dropping the soap into the sink.

"It's alright, Pixie. We're both going to have some

learning curves." He smiles before giving me a hug. "Come on, baby, get ready to go. We can talk more when we get home." I nod and pull back before he grabs my chin. "And don't think I will be forgetting about those ten spanks you have coming, little girl." I pout and he just chuckles, kissing me before leaving me to get dressed.

So, I know I was totally joking around with Daddy about wanting two Daddies because of the first book I read from Lana, but it was kind of hot.

I went back to the beginning of the author's Montana Daddies series and holy dang! Can I just say that I'm lucky to have my own cowboy Daddy?

Now I'm on to her Motorcycle Daddies series and holy shit!

"Umm, any chance you ride a motorcycle?" I look away from my kindle and at Travis. He stops working on whatever it is he has in front of him and gives me a quizzical look.

"No. Why?"

"No real reason." I smirk and look back to the

kindle. It's a super cute story about a rough and tough Dom who can't help but fall for his neighbour who happens to be a Little. It's beyond cute.

"I'm beginning to think I should be checking over those books Lana gave you to see if they're appropriate or not."

I gasp and hold the kindle to my chest, making him chuckle. "Mine." I pout and he laughs harder.

"Don't worry, Pixie. I won't take away your only source of entertainment while you're stuck here with me. Come here, baby." He moves his chair back and taps his leg.

Like the greedy girl I am, I close my kindle and practically knock him over with a hug before getting comfy.

"Hi Daddy," I whisper into his ear, and he sighs happily.

"I love when you call me that."

I smile and kiss his cheek. "Me too."

A knock on the door gets his attention.

Since I've been coming into work with him, he closes the blinds and keeps the door closed as well. He wants to make me feel as comfortable as possible.

"Come in." Trent walks into the room before closing the door.

"Sheriff, there's someone here to see you."

"Who is it?" Trent looks at me before moving his eyes to Travis and I get an uneasy feeling in the pit of my stomach.

"No one I know. Says they're here looking for their missing girlfriend." Aww, that's so sad. "He asked if we've seen anyone new around town and I said no, but he described—" He trails off and nods his head toward me, and Travis stiffens beneath me, his arms locking like a cage around me.

"Did you get a name?"

Trent nods again before looking back at me with an expression I can't decipher. "Chad Carleton."

I freeze. Shit, shit, shit!

"STARBURST!" I squeak out before covering my mouth, looking between them in fear.

"Huh?" Trent questions as Travis growls.

"Under the desk, Pixie. Not a sound, do you hear me? You're going to be alright. Keep a hand on me at all times and remember I will never let anything happen to you."

I nod and let him guide me under his desk. It's one of those old-fashioned ones where there's no space between the floor and the bottom, it's completely solid so no one can see underneath.

I shake violently as he quietly explains to Trent that it's my danger safeword.

I'm not sure what his reaction is, but before I know it, he opens the door and another set of footsteps comes in.

"Sheriff, thank you so much for taking the time to speak to me." I hear Chad's voice and I instantly feel the need to vomit.

At one point in time, I thought he was a really good guy and that he loved me. After months of being together, I gave him everything. My heart, my virginity, my trust. Everything…and it was a huge mistake.

Robert planted him in my life to try and control me. It took over a year before I found out that he was under my father's thumb and was just doing his bidding.

He used me and my innocent love for him as a way to keep tabs on everything I was doing.

God, that hurt so much when I found out.

When I broke up with him, I didn't even have the gall to face him after everything I had learned. I sent him a text and told him that I loved him, but I just couldn't be in a relationship anymore and then blocked his number.

I still have a hard time wrapping my head

around the conversation I overheard one night. Dad was furious about something that Chad and I had done, and Chad was explaining that it was the best way to gain my trust. That if I wanted to believe he actually loved me, he had to play the part of a doting boyfriend. That if he didn't, I would start asking questions and neither of them wanted that.

It's been over a year since I overheard them and it still hurts. Heartbreak sucks and knowing it was only ever one sided still makes me feel like a moron, but he was convincing as fuck.

"Not a problem." Travis clears his throat but doesn't make a move to get up. I squeeze his knee, closing my eyes and trying to control my breathing. "My deputy said you're looking for your girlfriend?"

There's something in his voice when he says girlfriend that makes me worried he might believe Chad's lies, so I squeeze his knee harder. He reaches his hand down to rest on my head in a calming gesture and I feel myself relax.

How he can read me so well after knowing me for just over a week is kind of freaky.

"Yes. She's mentally unstable and has run off before, but we can't find her. Her father and I are extremely worried." Chad's voice cracks with emotion, that's how genuine he sounds, and it makes me want to punch him in the dick.

Okay, violence is better than panic. Hold on to that, Rina!

"I'm truly sorry for the fear you guys are going through, but what can I do?" Gah, my Daddy is awesome. His voice is so stern and authoritative, I kind of want to jump him and ride him like a mechanical bull right now.

I wonder if they have one of those here? I could totally rock one of those bitches.

"I was just wondering if you could put out a flyer or town bulletin, or something maybe? Have someone call me if they see her?"

Aaannd the panic is back. He can't really say no to that, can he? Shit! If anyone sees my picture, they will know I'm here and who I'm staying with.

As if he knows what I'm thinking, he reaches back under the desk to stroke my hair until he feels me calming again.

"I can't put up flyers, but I can ask around for you. The flyers will worry and possibly scare the younger kids. My deputy informed me that you left her description with him?"

"I did, Sheriff. I understand that you want to do what is best for your town, but she is highly unstable. I need you to understand this isn't a normal missing person's case."

Ugh, you've got to be kidding me! He's such an asshole. I have BPD, not some sort of psychosis that has me out freaking murdering people! He's making me sound like Freddy Krueger or something. Sheesh.

"I do understand your concern, but I haven't seen anyone strange in our town for a while. I would notice a newcomer. We all would."

I tune out Chad's voice because if I don't, I'm going to lose my shit. I need something to distract me.

Looking around the small space under the desk, there is literally nothing here.

Crap! Why hadn't I brought the kindle over from the couch?

Because you wanted to sit on Daddy's lap. You didn't know your traitorous ex was going to come looking for you.

Biting my lip, I look at Travis' lap and decide I need to occupy myself, and since I don't have my books, there's only one option left.

Though, he may very well kill me when Chad leaves, but I need to do something. That cock-warming I read about isn't really my thing but sucking him off is something I've been wanting to do for days.

Every time we make out, I feel him against me, and I desperately want to touch him, but he wants to take it slow, and it may actually be killing me a little.

I'm not usually one to go all weak in the knees, but something about how manly he is just gets me so freaking hot I can't handle it.

I literally get myself off every night when he goes back to his room.

"Please, Sheriff. She's a very important girl to us." I almost lose control of the snort I want to give at that sentence.

Reaching into his lap, I grab the belt of his pants before he stiffens and reaches down to grip my hands in his to try and stop me.

I'm so not letting him stop me though.

"Mr. Carleton, I understand that she means a lot to you." I bet those words were hard to choke out. Good job, Daddy!

I lean over and lick the hand holding mine in place before biting him until he lets go. His hand moves to my hair, pulling on it roughly, and I feel myself getting soaked from the dominance.

"She means everything to me." I roll my eyes and start silently undoing his belt and jeans, stopping to frown at how tight they are. I can see his dick growing under my gaze, but I underestimated just how tight these damn things are on him.

Yes, they make his ass look fine as fuck, but this won't do.

His hand loosens a little on my hair when he thinks I've decided to give up.

Foolish Daddy.

I'm literally soaked and practically starving for his length now. There's no way I'm stopping.

"She means everything to you?" He parrots back and I lean forward, licking him through his jeans and feeling his hand tighten in my hair again, but instead of pulling me away, he holds me in place.

I smirk against him and take it as a win, using my tongue to travel up and down his bulge while Chad talks about my father and how much he loves me, and I'm glad my mouth is busy because I don't think I could stop the snort that wants to leave this time.

Travis goes to answer when I gently nip the length of him with my teeth and he lets out a quiet groan.

"Are you alright, Sheriff?" I hear Chad ask, and I want to laugh at the moron.

Travis clears his throat and lifts his hips like he's trying to get comfortable in his seat, but I know he's giving me the right amount of time to slide the jeans down just enough to pull his dick out.

Holy mother of Pearl. That is one thick dick.

Like, I'm not even kidding. The length is just above average, but holy shit, he's a thick boy.

"Fine. I just have a bit of a headache and had a sharp pain shoot through my temples." He pulls on my hair to pull my face closer to his dick and my eyes go wide.

Um, so I probably didn't think this through. Chad is the only guy I've ever been with, and he has a tiny pencil dick compared to Daddy.

I lean forward and lick the tip of his cock and his hand tightens even more in my hair.

Geez, he's going to give me a headache if he keeps that up. Do I care? Nah.

"I'm sorry to hear that." His voice sounds stupid, so I ignore him and start playing with Daddy's cock some more.

Travis

She's going to be the death of me.

What the fuck has gotten into her that made her want to take my dick out right this damn minute?

There are a million better times that this could have happened than when her scumbag ex is sitting across from me, pretending to be so concerned for her safety.

I tried to stop her, but seriously? I'm only human for fuck's sake, and I've been like a damn bottle rocket for the past week and a half since meeting her. Especially the past week since she called me Daddy and agreed to be mine.

I'll give it to the guy, his acting is pretty spot on. If I hadn't known how to read subtle body language, I would think he was truly concerned for her safety and in love with her.

Unfortunately for him, I'm excellent at reading people and his eyes are void of any emotion. He's detached and cold to the point I want to punch him.

I take a deep breath and calm my shit down after Rina's tongue touches the tip of my dick again, my hand tightening even more around her hair.

"It's quite alright. Paperwork." I shrug, playing off my earlier slip up to a migraine, but I know I'll lose control soon and I need to get him out of here. "I'm going to get Deputy Stevens to accompany you back to wherever you're staying, so he can get an accurate description and her details, and we will see what we can do." I try and keep my voice even as Rina lowers herself over me, swallowing when my crown hits her tonsils. I grit my teeth, pulling her hair to get her back off my dick because I can't take it, but she's being a brat and continues flicking her tongue against my crown.

I can feel the sweat dripping down my back as I fight to not stay silent.

"Thank you, Sheriff, I appreciate it." He stands up, giving me an odd look as to why I'm just reaching my hand over and not getting up to walk him out.

"You're more than welcome. I'm sorry I can't see you out right now, I have to get some things ready and head home." He nods before shaking my hand and walking out the door. "Could you please close that on your way out?" I point to my head, and he gives me a smile in understanding before closing the door.

I let go of her head and pull away from the desk and her whimper makes me smile.

"That was extremely naughty, Pixie." I look under my desk and almost blow my load seeing her swollen lips and mussed up hair.

Christ, she's perfect.

"I needed something to distract me, Daddy." She pouts, and it's fucking cute as hell, but I can see the truth in her eyes and nod.

Fixing myself until my jeans are done back up, I reach down and hold my hand out to her, walking her over to the couch, making sure the door is locked on the way in case that moron wants to come back.

"How are you doing with everything you heard?" I ask her, pulling her into my lap and snuggling close. I need to ignore my dick until I know she's okay. The last thing I want to do is upset her.

"Okay. Scared, pissed off, nauseous." She looks thoughtful before her face takes on a dark look I haven't seen before. "Who the hell does he think he is? Coming looking for me after what he did! Fucking asshole!" She grunts, and I want to correct her language, but not give her trouble for using in accordance with that slimy prick.

"I'm going to say this because of our little chat this morning." I start and she stiffens in my lap, her eyes searching mine. "Watch your language because the next time you swear, the time with the soap will be longer." Her nose does this cute scrunching thing that always happens when she thinks something is disgusting. "But when it comes to that prick, or either of your parents, I won't punish you for it."

She relaxes in my arms. "Thank you, Daddy."

I give her a small smile,

"You're welcome, Pixie girl." My phone vibrates in my pocket, and I pull it out to see a text from Trent.

> TRENT:
>
> He's staying in the place above Sammi's. You may want to take the long way around.

Fuck.

"Hey, Pixie?" She looks at me with worry and I sigh. I fucking hate how she's back on edge after having a good week.

"Yeah?"

"Let's go home, baby." I squeeze her and she gives me a sad smile and nods, getting up to pack up her kindle while I get my shit ready to go.

CHAPTER 12
TRAVIS

Quiet. That's the best word to describe how the afternoon and evening have been.

I've been giving Rina her space to try and process everything that happened today, but I don't want to give her too much time and have her wind up stuck in her head again.

Besides, someone needs a punishment for lying to me this morning.

I already decided not to punish her for being naughty when she played with my dick. She was just trying to distract herself, even if it nearly killed me.

"Pixie. Time to put the kindle away. We have some things to discuss." She lets out a dramatic sigh like being told to stop reading is a chore. I never imagined her as a book nerd, but she seems to pull everything off.

"Okay, Daddy. What's up?" She sits up on the leather chair across from the couch and looks at me.

"Come here, baby." I tap my lap and she smiles before getting a nervous look as she gets closer. I think she just remembered her punishment.

"Umm..."

I shake my head and she grumbles, sitting down on me. "Talk first, hot bottom after."

She gives me this puppy dog look that makes me almost want to forget it, but I can't. I haven't been the Daddy she's needed this week, and I need to show her I will follow through with punishment when breaking the rules because she needs that consistency.

"Daddy, I really don't think the spanking is necessary. Today was a crummy day already, right? I kind of want to jump to the fun part of the night." I watch her squirm with amusement.

"And what part is that, Pixie girl?"

"Sex." And there goes the control of my dick.

"That's one of the things I wanted to talk to you about. How do you feel about what happened in the office?"

She bites her lip and I groan. God, she's beautiful.

"I loved it and I want more. Daddy, I got so wet just seeing you." She blushes. I love how her cheeks flare against her pale skin when she's embarrassed.

"Oh yeah? You want more, huh?" She giddily claps her hands, nodding her head.

"Yes please."

I smirk and kiss the tip of her nose.

"Why don't we see how you take your first spanking? Normally, I wouldn't reward you with an orgasm after a punishment, but I'm not sure either of us can wait."

"Yeah, Daddy, I don't want to wait."

I snort and help her stand up. "You aren't getting out of your punishment, Pixie girl. Pants and undies off."

She blushes and bites her lip before following what I say.

Watching her bend and undress is almost my undoing.

Her ass cheeks are tiny handfuls that I want to grip and slap while I fuck her and make her scream.

"Is this okay?" she asks, looking nervous about being naked from the waist down.

"Why wouldn't it be?" I tap my thighs and help

her lay on her belly so her perfect little ass is open for me. "You're gorgeous, Rina." My palm lands on the soft globes and she squeals.

"I've only ever been with one guy before. I'm not really used to this." I really don't know how to react to that.

On the one hand, that means she's inexperienced and I get to show her the pleasure and love that comes from this type of relationship. On the other, it means she screwed that slimy piece of shit from earlier today, and my desire to kill him is even higher.

"Thank you for telling me, Pixie. I promise to go at your pace. We can go as slow as you need to." And I will, even if my dick isn't exactly on board with waiting.

"No. No going slow. You've been practically killing me this past week." She wiggles on my lap, her stomach pressing against my bulge.

Slapping her cheek playfully, she whimpers, and I feel myself jerk.

"You've been suffering this week?" I know she has. I also know she's gotten herself off at least once every night because the walls are thin, and the sounds of her moans have had me on edge for days. My hand just isn't enough to get my dick to chill out.

"You know I have. You have to know!" she whines and I chuckle, moving my hand over her sweet bubble butt.

"Yeah, baby, I know. I just wanted to make sure you were ready." I cough to clear my throat of the desire and need coursing through my veins. "Your actions in the office earlier prove that you are."

Her ass wiggles against my hand. "I am."

I nod before turning serious again.

"Good girl for telling me the truth. Now we have to take care of your punishment for lying to Daddy."

I see her swallow. "I'm sorry." She's already sniffling, and it makes my chest ache.

"I know you are, Pixie, but you made a valid point this morning. I've been treating you with kid gloves when I shouldn't have been. If I can't show follow through, how will you ever be able to trust me?"

She mumbles under her breath, something about being stupid and too talkative or some bullshit.

"That's five more. You're up to fifteen. Want to keep going?"

She gasps, trying to sit up but my hand goes to the small of her back to keep her in place."Fifteen?! What for?!"

"You called yourself stupid just now. If I'm not going to let anyone else hurt you, what makes you think you're allowed?" I ask her, and she scrunches her nose in confusion.

"But I didn't hurt myself."

"You did mentally. Even if you didn't have a mental health disorder, I would never allow you to talk badly about yourself. But you do have mental health issues, Rina, and I won't let you drive yourself into self-hate. I know it's a pattern for BPD sufferers."

She sniffs. "You've really done that much reading up on it?" She seems genuinely shocked, and it makes me angry at the people in her life up to this point. Again.

At this rate, I want to just rid the world of them all.

"Of course. I told you I took your health and safety seriously and I meant it."

She smiles through tears. "Thank you." I rub her back. "Can we get this over with now, please?" Such a sassy pants.

"Yeah, Pixie, we can. Remind me what your safe word is if you need anything to stop." She lets out a breath.

"Red."

"Good girl. Here they are."

I don't give her a chance to tense up before my hand lands on her cheeks, back and forth in a repeated motion for the first five.

"Colour, Pixie?" She moves around, trying to ease the ache in her pink cheeks and grumbling.

"Green, I guess. But my butt hurts, Daddy! I learned my lesson, I swear!"

I shake my head.

"Then the last ten will solidify that in your mind, won't they? They will help you to remember the next time you think about lying or putting yourself down."

I rapid fire five more, her bottom turning a nice red as she starts sobbing in my arms and trying to wriggle free.

"No more, Daddy! It hurts, I'm sorry! I won't do it again!" Her sobs tug at my heart, but I can't stop. I know she needs this reminder and the feeling of the guilt being let go.

"You're doing great, Pixie. You have five more and then everything is forgiven," I remind her because I'm positive the people in her life have always held shit against her even after a punishment. I want to show her that a better life exists outside of those assholes.

"You... you promise?" she cries more, and I rub my hand over her heated ass.

"I promise you, Rina. Five more. Can you do that for Daddy?" She pauses and sniffles before nodding her head. "Good girl. Last five are going to be harder alright?"

Five more swats later, I'm pulling up a sobbing girl into my lap, cuddling her close to me with words of praise and love.

"You were such a good girl, taking your punishment for Daddy. I'm proud of you, baby." I kiss her head as she sniffs into my shirt, tears still running down her face.

"I'm so sorry, Daddy! I won't do it again, I promise. I don't want to lie to you." She hiccups through the sobs, and I nod, quieting her with comfort.

"Shh, I know. It's okay, Pixie girl, I've got you."

After she's calmed down a bit, I pull her away from my chest to look into her eyes.

God, she's so beautiful.

"How about a bath?" I ask her, and she does this cute little head tilt.

"I thought you were going to fuck me, Daddy." Holy fucking shit. Is she trying to kill me? Like really! I'm just trying to help her feel better first.

"We can, but I figured we could take a bath together first. Help you relax a bit after crying?"

She nods her head, a soft smile on her face. "Sure, if you're joining me!" Fuck, she's adorable.

"You got it, Pixie girl." I wink at her, moving her around until she's straddling me. Standing up, her legs automatically wrap around my waist, and I head to the bathroom, kissing her forehead as I go.

I know the spanking turned her on because I can feel the wetness of her core against me right now, and it's taking everything to keep my shit together.

I purposely didn't touch or look at the perfect pussy calling to me because I knew I would unravel so damn fast.

There will be time for that later. Right now, I want to take care of her.

Setting her down on the counter beside the sink, I help her strip off the rest of her clothes before doing the same with mine.

Her eyes travel over my body with hunger, and I'm so fucking tempted to say fuck the bath instead of turning it on, but I don't. It's her first spanking and the warm water will feel good on her hot little ass.

Moving away, I turn the tub on before moving back in front of her, cupping her cheek in my hand. She leans into my touch and smiles.

"You're my every wish come true," she whispers, tears rimming her eyes again and I feel myself getting emotional.

"And you, my sweet and sassy Pixie girl, are everything I never knew I needed." I give her a huge smile before leaning in to kiss her softly.

Her arms and legs immediately pull me into her until my dick rubs against her wet core and I groan, gripping her hips and deepening the kiss. Our tongues meet and worship each other as we push and pull, trying to get the best leverage to take the kiss deeper.

She's claiming me as hers and branding my heart forever with the feel of her touch just as much as I am her.

I moan, pulling away from her swollen lips to shut the tub off. When I turn back to her, her eyes are glazed over and glossy, pupils dilated, and I know I'm fucked.

There will never be another woman for me because I will never forget how she looks right now in this moment.

"Come on, Pixie. Let's get into the warm water." She lets out a dreamy sigh as I help her off the sink before picking her up and lowering us both into the tub together.

. . .

Rina

This has to be what heaven feels like. I don't think I've ever felt as loved and safe as I do in Travis' arms right now and I know for a fact I never want to leave.

Heck, even the town is growing on me this past week and a half. If it means staying here in Haven Hills with him, I would choose the country bumpkin life in a heartbeat.

"What just crossed your mind, Pixie girl?" he asks, studying my face as I sit in his lap, the warm water surrounding us.

"Just wondering what happens when this is all over. If I survive my father."

He growls and grabs my chin in a fierce grip.

"You will fucking survive because I'm not losing you after just finding you. You get me, Pixie?" His fierce tone has my core flooding, clenching with desire, and he groans.

"Yes, Daddy." Pulling my chin, he brings my mouth to his before moving his hands into my hair.

I easily give into him, letting him rule me with

his hands, his mouth, and his dominance. Fuck, it's the hottest thing I've ever felt in my life.

A kiss has never felt so hot and demanding before. I've kissed a few guys, but even with Chad, things were never this hot and intense.

I moan into his lips, making him grunt and move his hands down my body to play with my breasts, squeezing the nipples between his thumb and forefinger.

"Please, Daddy," I whimper, moving my core until I'm on top of his thickness.

"Baby, we should move this to the bed." But I shake my head, moving my hand between us to grip his length and he jerks at my touch. "Ah fuck," he hisses out against my lips, and I smile.

"I want you now, Daddy. Right here, like this," I whisper, and he groans.

His hands move to my hips, rubbing me against his erection until I feel like I'm going to lose my mind if I don't feel him inside me.

I've never wanted anything as badly as I want him right now.

"Condom. Ah, Christ," he curses as his tip slides past my entrance.

"I have an IUD and I'm clean. Chad was the only one," I tell him in a whisper.

"I'm clean, too, Pix but are you—FUCK!" he growls as I drop myself down his length and holy shit, he feels good.

The stretch of his thickness causes a slight burning, but having him inside of me is incredible. "Fucking hell, Pix. Warn a guy." He breathes hard, eyes closed, and I giggle, kissing his jaw.

"Sorry, Daddy, I couldn't wait."

He groans, his hands squeezing my hips before moving back to my ass, lifting me up a little and guiding me back down, making us both moan.

"Fuck, baby. You feel so good. So fucking tight for me," he grinds out, lifting my hips and thrusting up into me, making the water splash around us.

"Yes," I moan, and dig my nails into his shoulders as he picks up speed, thrusting into me from below, hard and fast as the water splashes out the sides of the tub. I don't even care.

"So good, baby. Mine, all fucking mine."

I moan, leaning in to kiss his lips, circling my hips and grinding against him until my pulse is racing, my body feeling like it's going to explode but I don't want it to end.

"So good. So good, Daddy. Harder please!" I scream against his lips, and his fingers dig into my ass so hard I know they're going to leave bruises.

"You want it harder, Pixie?" he taunts, and I whimper.

"Please!" My hips are circling and trying to move against his grip, but he stills us both and I feel like I'm going to cry, I'm so on the edge.

"Then say it, Rina. Say you're mine and you aren't going anywhere." His eyes are hard, searching mine, and I whimper again. Seeing the heat and determination in them is a heady mixture.

"Yours. Only yours. Please, Travis!"

He moves us so quickly, more water splashes out of the bath as he bends me over the side before sliding in behind me.

"Hold on, Pix. This is going to get rough." He thrusts into me, forcing my body forward on a scream.

"Oh, God!" I shout as he pounds into me over and over again, tripping every nerve on his way in, and hitting just the right spot on the way out.

"That's it, baby. Take my cock until you're screaming your release. I want to feel you gripping me so hard I have to cum with you."

I moan, unable to form words as his hand comes around my neck, turning my head at an odd angle before his lips descend on mine. He doesn't slow down as his tongue battles mine for dominance while his other hand curls under me, squeezing my clit and I'm off like a rocket.

"Oh, my God, YES!!!!" I scream, closing my eyes as white light explodes behind my eyelids, my entire body shaking with the most powerful orgasm I've ever felt.

"That's it, Pixie girl. Squeezing me so fucking tight. FUCK!" he grinds out. His hips stop thrusting but still moves in circles as I feel his hot cum jet into me.

Whimpering as my soul floats back into my body, I open my eyes.

Travis is trying to hold himself up and not crush me as he catches his breath. He looks at me watching him and smiles before pulling out slowly and I pout, making him chuckle.

"Don't worry. That will not be the only time we do that." Well, thank fuck for that.

"Okay," I say, before yawning and he chuckles some more before helping me to stand and get out of the tub.

Handing me a towel, he leans down to let the water go before taking the towel from me and drying us both off, pulling me into a tight hug.

"How are you feeling, baby?" he asks, pulling back a bit to watch me and I smile.

"So good. Sore, but good," I say before yawning again. Picking me up, he heads towards the door before I remember. "Daddy?"

"Yeah, Pixie?"

"Mess."

"What?"

"Splisshhhhhh." I make a movement of my hand to mimic the water splashing over the sides of the tub, and he freezes.

"Shit. Right. Hang on a sec." He moves back into the room and lowers me to the counter beside the sink before moving to clean up the water we got literally everywhere.

When he's done, he picks me up again and carries me to my room.

The disappointment is there but doesn't last longer than a moment before he picks up Circuit and takes me to his room, sliding me under the covers and joining me.

"Okay, back on topic. Are you sore from the punishment, or the sex? Was I too rough?" I can see the worry on his face even though it's dark in here.

"Mainly the spanking, but it's a good sore. You fucked me just right, Daddy." I snuggle into his chest, tangling our legs together and he sighs.

"I should give you trouble for swearing, but I will

let it slide when you're talking about sex. Deal?" He kisses my head and I giggle, nodding.

"Super dealio." I fall asleep to the feeling of his body moving as he laughs and whispers something about me being adorable.

CHAPTER 13
RINA

I CANNOT GET ENOUGH OF THE GOOD SHERIFF, BOTH IN and out of bed and it's all his fault. He's made me feel secure and happy and now my brat is showing and it's driving him crazy.

"Rina!" he bellows from his office, and I giggle, running past Trent to hide before he catches me. "Get that pretty little ass back here right now, Pixie!"

"No running!" Trent hollers at me, and yeesh, the dude is no fun. Seriously, he's trying to be a killjoy.

Nope, not happening.

I keep moving, running to the back room where I was in lock up that first night and look around. I need to hide. Where oh where can I hide that doesn't involve one of those cells? Because ick. I remember that smell and no, thank you!

"I'm going to count to three, Pixie girl, and if you don't come out here, you're going over my knee in front of everyone." Oh, crapadoodle. He totally would too.

"That's not fair!" I stomp my foot and squeak before realizing I just gave myself away, and I can hear both men chuckling.

Such turdbutts.

"Did she just call us turdbutts?" Trent asks incredulously, and I slap myself in the forehead.

Crap! I did not mean to say that out loud.

"I think she did. Don't think she meant to say it out loud, though," Daddy says as he walks into the back room, and I'm frozen to the spot.

"Uh, Daddy? I can explain." My voice is higher pitched than normal, so he definitely knows I'm in little space.

It took a bit for me to get used to flowing in and out of little space with ease and not caring who is around when it's Trent and Lana. Turns out she's a Little too, which is really cool.

"You can explain to me why there's honey all over my ass? Do tell, Pixie."

I start giggling before the laughter takes over so much, I have to grip my tummy. "All the better to eat you with?" I choke out through laughter, and he stops moving.

"Did you just compare yourself to the big bad wolf?"

"Me? No, never. Why would I do a thing like that?" I straighten myself, still silently laughing at the look on his face before making minuscule steps to get into a better position for me to run past him.

"Hmm, I don't know. Hey, Trent!"

"Yeah?" He can barely contain his laughter from the next room, and I roll my eyes.

"Why would a certain little girl compare herself to the big bad wolf?"

Trent starts laughing and hollers back. "My guess? She thinks she's tougher than her big bad Daddy."

My eyes widen as Daddy smirks at me.

"No! I—I, uh..." Shoot.

Think, Rina, think!

"You, uh what, Pixie?" he taunts, taking another step toward me, and I move another step back.

"I definitely didn't think I was tougher than you, Daddy. You're super strong, and handsome, and epic-ness!" I nod my head with every word. The smirk never falls off his face as he keeps advancing on me.

"Super strong, handsome, and epicness, huh?" I nod my head harder, taking more steps back until I'm against the cell bars and groan. Dang it! Swallowing, I look at him warily which only makes his grin grow. "Uh-huh." I look around him and decide to try and dart to his left, but he catches me with his arm around my waist and I squeak. "No, Daddy!" I start laughing as his hands come around my waist, tickling me until I fall to the ground laughing.

"What's that, Pixie? The big bad Daddy can't hear you," he teases, and I laugh harder, snorting as he attacks my sides with vigour.

"I'm sorry! You're the bestest, biggest Daddy ever!" I squeal until I feel like I'm going to pee. "I gonna pee my pants, Daddy, stop!" I groan, laughing through his tickle assault until he stops and smiles down at me.

"Are you ever going to put honey, or any other substance, on Daddy's chair again?" I shake my head, still trying to catch my breath from the tickle attack. "Good girl," he says, getting off me before helping me to stand up, my breath still coming fast.

"Thank you, Daddy." I give him a smile and wrap my arms around his waist, squeezing as tight as I can until he grunts, his arms wrapping around me.

"For what, Pix?" He kisses my head and I sigh into him.

"For being everything. I–I think I'm in love with you," I whisper the last part, and he stills.

"Say that again?" I can't tell if he's angry or not, but I'm also scared to lose him, so I shake my head. "Yes, Pixie. Say it again." He pulls back, leaning down until his nose is touching mine and I close my eyes.

"I think I'm in love with you."

He grins and kisses me softly. "That's good, because I think I'm in love with you, too." He winks but I frown.

"You think? Shouldn't *you* know?" I ask, narrowing my eyes and he lifts an eyebrow at me.

"Shouldn't you?"

I blow out a breath and roll my eyes.

"I've never been in real love before, but what I feel for you is a billion, trillion times more potent than how I felt about Chad."

Daddy growls and pulls me against him while looking into my eyes.

"Fuck, Chad. He never deserved your love, but I'm glad to know you feel a billion, trillion times more for me." He winks and then kisses me again before pulling away. "I've never been in love either,

Pixie. But I imagine the fact I never want to be away from you is a dead giveaway to my love for you."

"It is!" Trent hollers from the other room, and we both laugh.

"Thank you, oh wise one," Travis hollers back and, I snort.

"Anytime, boss." We can hear the glee in his voice, and I wrap my arms around his waist again before pulling away.

"How much longer until we go home?" I ask, and he smiles.

"Actually, Ethan should be here soon and then we're going to Serenity." I clap and jump on the balls of my feet.

"Yay! I get to see Lana and the horses!" He smiles and holds his hand out for me to take and I do.

I'd follow him anywhere.

Travis

"Look at them," Trent chuckles from beside me, and I just smile.

"It's incredible to see them both happy."

His face darkens before nodding. "They both deserve it." He lets out a small growl that dissipates the moment the girls giggle. "Any luck finding the son of a bitch yet?"

I let out a sigh. "No. I have to do it so far under the radar that it's impossible to get anything done."

He looks thoughtful. "I can get my partner in Omaha to run him and the boyfriend. See if anything pops up?"

I think about it and the dangers of having them run the names instead of us. It's five hours away and there are no official records of his connection with Serenity Stables, but Chad saw him in the station.

"No." I shake my head and he looks at me like I'm daft. "Don't look at me like that. Chad saw you at the station and he's still in town. He's going to recognize your name and photo in their system the second he sees it. We can't risk Serenity Stables like that before it even gets off the ground. You guys are weeks from opening." He lets out a sigh and nods. "And I will never put Rina in that kind of danger. She wouldn't be fucking terrified for her life if these pricks weren't serious."

He looks at me for a second before turning back

to the girls. "I owe you a lot for saving Lana," he says, and I wave it off.

"It's my job to make sure assholes like that don't harm good people."

He snorts. "Pretty sure you mean it's your job to serve and protect the people of the town."

I purse my lips and narrow my eyes at him. "Same thing."

He actually laughs. "Sure, boss. You keep telling yourself that and if you ever need a favour from me, just ask." He gets serious as the girls walk over to us. "She's my everything, and I would have done it myself if you hadn't. You saved her."

I don't get a chance to respond before Rina is standing in front of me, looking at me with wide eyes.

"You alright, Pixie girl?" I feel my heart beating in my chest as she blinks at me before Lana starts giggling like a schoolgirl.

"She's fine. Just had a little... um... accident?" Rina glares at her, and I share a look with Trent.

"What do you mean, accident? Are you okay?" I start feeling her for injuries. "I thought you were putting her on a safe horse for beginners!" I snap at Trent and Lana falls over herself laughing while

Rina blushes so badly I feel like she's not even breathing.

"I let her ride Cocoa. You know how perfectly safe he is. He's a good boy." I let out a breath, confusion running through me when I remember we've been watching them the whole time.

Lana is experienced with horses and if anything had happened, I'd have seen Rina get hurt.

"Right. Then what happened?" Rina looks so scared and embarrassed that I take pity on her. "Can you whisper it to Daddy?"

She lets out the breath she was holding and nods before motioning me to bend down to her level.

Leaning forward she cups her hand around my ear. "I may have had a mini orgasm."

My eyes widen as I think of what to say. I know I can't laugh, but fuck. She's so scared that she had an orgasm in front of others, I don't even know how to respond.

She pulls away to look at my face, searching to see if I'm angry.

"It's okay, Pix," I tell her, and she relaxes her shoulders.

"I just... I know that it's weird," she whispers, and I smile.

"It's not that unheard of, Pixie girl. Especially

with how worked up you've been lately." I wink and she blushes again before looking back at Lana.

"Sorry if that was weird."

Lana throws her arms around my girl and giggles.

"Totally okay. It's happened to me before, too. Daddy likes to control mine and sometimes I get so worked up, the smallest thing sets me off."

Trent looks smug as hell when I glance at him, and I don't blame him. Controlling your sub's orgasms is a serious high and I'd love to get there with Rina when all of this is over, but I know she's not there yet.

She needs to have more control in her life before I take that away from her too. It's not punishment because I will make her cum eventually, but I want her to seek her own pleasure first. Though…

"Maybe we should try that, Pixie girl. What do you think?" She gasps, turning so fast that she almost topples over before I catch her. "Easy, baby." I shake my head at her and her eyes narrow.

"You… you want to control my pleasure?" she hisses, but it's not quiet enough for just me to hear. Thankfully Trent is a good sport about keeping quiet.

"In slow increments. We can talk about it more at

home." I give her a pointed look and she blushes again.

Groaning, she covers her face in her hands. "Shoot me," she grumbles, and I move her hands away from her face.

"There is nothing to be embarrassed about. They're in the lifestyle too, and it sounds like you have an easier time in that current category than Lana does. Right?"

She sighs and nods before looking at me with imploring eyes.

"You're right." She yawns and then slaps her hand over her mouth.

"Tired?" I lift an eyebrow and she shakes her head hard while leaving her hand over her mouth.

"No." Comes out muffled and Trent laughs.

"Are you guys staying for dinner?" he asks, and I look at Rina to gauge how she's feeling before pulling her into my side.

"I don't think so. Not tonight at least. I need to get this one home." She sags against me with relief, and I know I made the right call.

She's not one to tell me how she feels because she's worried it goes against what I want, but I know she can only handle so much socializing at a time.

The information Derek sent me on Borderline

Personality Disorder has come in handy when learning about her quirks, triggers, and upsets. Especially when she's not always able to voice them.

I'm not a specialist by any means, but I am patient and willing to learn and go with the flow. And I think as a support system for her, that's half the battle. The rest is knowledge and love. All of which I have for her in spades.

Trent must see the relief in her eyes because he gives me a curt nod before we say our goodbyes and get in the truck to head home.

CHAPTER 14
RINA

THERE'S ALWAYS A MOMENT WHEN YOU REALIZE THAT everything in your life could very well come crashing down. And in my case, it happens around the three week mark of my being in Haven Hills.

Things were going so well with Travis, and I had made a true and genuine friend. I was happy for the first time in my life, but nothing lasts forever.

"Well, well, well." I freeze at the sound of his voice, grasping on to my Daddy for dear life, because adult me? She left the building the second his sleezy voice crept into my mind. "If it isn't my long-lost girl-friend," Chad taunts from behind us.

"Ex," I whisper, and he cackles. It's a truly evil sound. How had I not seen how deranged he was sooner?

"Aww, baby, don't be like that." Travis is stiff against me before pulling my front against his chest so I don't have to see Chad when he turns us around.

"You have no reason to still be in my town. It's very clear she wants nothing to do with you, Chad."

I hear my ex snort, but stay close to my safe place, pulling him tighter against me.

"Come now, Sheriff. I told you how unstable she is. I really think it's best you let me take her home where her father and I can care for her." I feel him stiffen beneath me even more if that's possible.

"I know what you said, but I've come to know her and according to the doctor here, she's perfectly fine." I definitely melt a little with how easily he comes to my defence.

"I don't think a small-town doctor has the correct qualifications to assess her mental state. She needs strict professional help, Sheriff." I can hear the edge of annoyance in his voice. He's not used to people going against him, and it's showing.

"Maybe not, but I've also been in contact with a more than qualified psychiatrist. She's in good hands here." Daddy is doing a good job at staying calm, but I can feel the anger vibrating through him. I turn my head to stare down one of the people threatening my life.

"Go away, Chad. I'm not leaving with you or leaving here. Not ever." Daddy kisses my head before looking back at the threat.

"You heard her. I think it's time you left here and didn't come back." He takes out his phone and holds it to his ear. "We're a few doors down, Trent. I need you to escort Mr. Carleton out of town. He's no longer welcome in Haven Hills." He hangs up.

"Not a very wise move, Sheriff. Keeping her here is just putting everyone else in danger. You should just let me take her home where she belongs." A shiver of fear runs through me as I hold off the whimper that wants to escape, and Daddy's arms tighten around me in reassurance.

"Is that a threat?" Daddy all but growls, and Chad holds his hands up in mock surrender.

"Just an observation. He's never going to stop looking for her, and I'm not going to keep it from him. Robert Flemming isn't the kind of man you keep secrets from. Not if you want to live." Before he can answer, Trent pulls up in a police cruiser and steps out.

"Mr. Carleton, I'm going to have to ask you to come with me so we can get your stuff, and I will see you out of town."

Chad scowls at all of us before throwing up his hands. "Fine. But don't say I didn't warn you!"

Once Trent and Chad leave, Daddy picks me up and carries me back to his truck before buckling me into the passenger seat and climbing in on his own side of the truck, sliding over until he's right beside me.

"How are you holding up, Pixie girl?" He kisses the side of my head, wrapping his arms around me in a tight side hug. "I'm so fucking proud of you, baby."

"I—I don't know what to do," I whisper, staring straight ahead. I am so afraid of what he and Robert will do to Travis and everyone in this town.

"What do you mean, Pixie girl?" I take a shuddering breath as the tears strain the back of my eyes.

"He's right. Anything that happens from this point on is my fault. You're going to get hurt b-because of... me." I start crying, the tears and sobs shaking my body and he holds me close, comforting me like I'm not about to be the reason he gets killed. "He's going to kill you and make me watch before he kills me!" I scream, shaking so hard and trying to fight him.

I need to leave. To run and never stop so that the people I've come to love don't die because of me. It's better to be alone and heartbroken while they live, than to be the reason they die.

"Hey, now. No one is dying, Pixie. You need to breathe, baby. I promise you that you're safe."

"You, you can't promise that!" I scream and cry harder, and he growls, grabbing my face in his hands so he's looking through my tears and right into my soul.

"I can and I fucking will! No one is going to touch you, and we're going to stay at Serenity to make sure of it."

I keep crying, but confusion slows the tears. "No! We can't put them at risk too!"

He gives me a scary kind of smile before kissing my lips hard and fast.

"There's something you don't know about Serenity, but it's the safest place we can be right now. Trust me to protect you, Rina." He tightly holds my face, searching my eyes.

I sniff, the tears still falling. "I love you so much. I just don't want anything to happen to you." He kisses me gently. "I do trust you. I've never trusted anyone the way I do you. You're my Daddy."

"And you're my sweet Pixie girl. I will never let them hurt you. I promise." I search his eyes, trying to find anything that would make him unsure, but there's nothing there aside from determination and an over-pouring of love.

"Okay. Okay, I won't leave," I whisper, and he pulls me in for one more kiss before moving back to his side of the truck and taking us to pack up everything we need from his place.

"Oh, Katrina, I'm going to love taking your very last breath from you." Dad taunts me as I'm tied up to a chair in the middle of some warehouse.

"No," I whimper, and he laughs.

"Yes. If my parents wanted to make sure I didn't get any more of their money, they shouldn't have left it to you. They knew what they were doing. They were signing your life over to me."

No, Grandma and Grandpa wouldn't do that to me. They wouldn't. "You're lying."

He shakes his head as if he's disappointed in me.

"Such a naïve little bitch. Just like your mother." He stalks towards me, knife in hand, ready to kill me so he can gain access to my trust fund.

"No. Please don't hurt me." His cackles ring through my ears as his face grows more and more vicious the closer he gets.

"Rina, wake up! Wake up!" I startle awake with my arms wrapped around my waist, and scream.

"No! Get away from me. Don't touch me! Leave me alone, please! Please, don't hurt me!"

"It's alright, Pixie. You're safe with Daddy. You're safe. We're at Serenity Stables, remember?"

"No, you're going to hurt me. I don't trust you!"

"Shh, baby. I'd never hurt you, Pixie girl. Come back to me now, baby."

Daddy... "Daddy?"

He pulls me tight. "Yeah, Pix. It's me."

"Daddy...don't let him hurt me. Don't let him hurt you," I beg, and he pulls me into his lap.

"I've got you, baby. Nightmare?"

I nod, crying into his neck. "Sometimes they're so real. Please don't leave me," I whisper and he shudders, holding me tighter.

"I'm never leaving you, Pixie girl. I promise." He kisses the top of my head, soothing me until my tears stop falling.

All that's left is the exhaustion I feel from the day and being woken from a nightmare.

"I just want it all to stop," I whisper, yawning into his neck and he nods.

"I know, baby. Get some sleep now." He grabs Circuit off the bed and hands him to me to snuggle with as he lays us back down.

He doesn't have to tell me twice.

Travis

We're both tired as fuck as we sit down at the table for breakfast in the main house.

When we arrived late last night, I hadn't even thought about getting food at the grocery store. I was more concerned with getting Rina somewhere safe and helping her to relax.

Not that it helped much if her nightmare was any indication.

"So, whose cabin are we staying in?" Rina looks between Lana, Trent and I, and I wince. I had meant to tell her all about Serenity Stables yesterday, but I didn't want to overwhelm her with a bunch of information.

"You haven't told her yet?" I hear Carl ask from the kitchen and groan.

Carl Easton is the oldest of Lana's brothers and a couple of years older than me. He also happens to run Serenity and the operations right alongside Trent and myself.

"Didn't get the chance." I give Pixie an apologetic look.

"No time like the present," Lana chirps, making Rina giggle. My chest eases a bit seeing her smiling so soon after everything.

"Well, it's more your story to tell, anyway. Why don't you tell Rina all about your plan?" I give Lana a smile, and Trent nods at me in thanks.

Not that I would ever tell Lana's story without her permission, but Serenity Stables becoming such a safe place for others was her genius idea, and I think it will mean more to Rina if she hears it from her friend.

"Okay." She turns to Rina and claps her hands. "Well, my dad started Serenity Stables for our mom. She was bipolar and he knew that horses were what made her the happiest, so Serenity was created." She shrugs before sharing a look with her brothers, one of love and remembrance. "Anyway, my ex-boyfriend tried to kill me last year."

My girl gasps as tears rim her eyes for her friend, and Lana grabs her hand.

"Are you okay? Is he dead?" She narrows her eyes at the last question with a fury on her face that I haven't seen, and Lana nods.

"He is, but we will get to that another time." Lana clears her throat of emotion. "Anyway, I moved back home to start over and realized just how soothing it can be here away from the world."

"You said that the first night we met," Rina says, and Lana smiles at her.

"I did, and I think you see it now, too."

Rina nods before Lana continues telling her story as Trent, Carl, and I sit back and watch the girls.

"Anyway, after a billion failed counselling attempts, Sheriff set me up with his brother, Derek, and he actually helped me heal."

Rina looks at me with soft eyes and I give her a small smile. I see the question in her eyes, so I answer it.

"You can talk to him whenever you want to, Pixie girl. As my brother, or as a psychiatrist, with absolutely no judgement." She sniffs and nods at me before turning back to her new best friend.

"After a while, I decided I wanted to go back to school for social work and counselling. I decided that we should make Serenity Stables a place to help others heal, so that's what we've been working toward."

Carl is the one to jump in next. "We had a few cabins built with top-of-the-line security, and the security gate is being installed later this week. It's the last thing we need before we officially open for business."

Rina looks confused. "So, why so much security if it's just for rebuilding their lives?" They all look to me to respond.

"Because Lana decided that she wants Serenity to be about protecting not only abuse survivours, but anyone that may be in danger. If someone is here to hide because they witnessed a murder, they need the protection." I take a deep breath before continuing.

"She wants this to be a place to come to where they can just disappear and be safe until the people after them are caught. Trent is actually a detective with the Omaha Police Department as well as my deputy," I explain.

"There are a lot of laws and red tape to keep

something like this place hidden with no paper trail connected to the police, but we want everyone to feel safe here, so the added security measures are a bonus." I watch her as I finish explaining, waiting for her response.

"Wow. That's... thank you for letting me be a part of it, and for letting me stay here." Her eyes fill with tears and I stand to grab her, but Lana has pulled her into a tight hug before I can even move.

"You're always welcome here, bestie!"

Trent snorts and smiles while Carl shakes his head before heading back to the door.

"If you guys need to leave for any reason, give one of us a call, and we will come back to watch the girls." Trent and I share a look and nod before he leaves.

"You're leaving me?" Rina looks panicked and I sigh.

"No, baby. Not unless there's an absolute emergency."

She sighs with relief and Lana pulls her up.

"Want to colour with me?" Rina's eyes go wide, looking at me for approval, and I nod.

"Go ahead, if you want to. As long as Trent is alright with that."

He snorts beside me. "I'm fine with it. Lana

colours every morning after breakfast before she dives into her schoolwork. Helps her clear her mind."

And just like that, the girls take off to the table in the living room with Trent and I both hollering for them to stop running. It's going to be a good day.

CHAPTER 15
RINA

Colouring was a lot more fun than I realized it could be.

After we were done, Lana went to do her online schoolwork while Travis decided to take me for a walk around the ranch. They have acres upon acres of land that I'm dying to walk through.

Before I came here, I swore up and down that I hated the small-town country life, but it's grown on me. I can see its appeal now that I've spent some time here.

Everything slows down, and you can actually breathe instead of rushing to try and do a million different things at once.

Unlike in the city, there is a peace and tranquility here that I didn't even realize I needed in my life.

"What are you thinking about, Pix?" Travis squeezes my hand, and I sigh.

"Did you know I detested country life when I arrived here?"

He snorts. "Yeah, Pix. You made that pretty clear in all of your smart-ass comments."

I roll my eyes and he pulls me close, tickling me until I snort out laughter and beg for mercy.

"I'm sorry!" I laugh and he stops, pulling me over to the tree closest to us and pressing me against it.

"You're sorry, hmm, Pixie?" I swallow when he presses closer against me, feeling his hardness against my stomach.

"Most definitely sorry." I look into his eyes, giving him the most innocent expression I can muster, and he chuckles.

"Somehow, I don't believe you." I start to laugh, but his mouth crashes against mine and I moan into him, my arms wrapping around his neck.

His kiss is filled with love, heat, and need, and I am right there with him, giving it back as good as I'm getting.

"Daddy," I moan into his mouth, and he trails kisses down my jaw and neck.

"God, I want you, Pix. I always want you so

fucking badly," he groans, his hips pushing against me.

"Then take me," I whisper.

He groans, pulling back to look me in the eyes as desire and heat darken his. "You know we rarely have sex in a bed, right?"

I snort and shrug. "I don't care where we have sex as long as I get you inside me as quickly as possible. Besides, beds are overrated, old man." I wink and he's done after that.

"Is that so? Then get ready to be fucked up against this tree, Pix. Turn around." He bites my lip before quickly turning me, so my chest is against the tree. "Is this what you want, Pixie? You want me to fuck you against this tree?"

I moan and nod, turning my head to look at him. He growls, lunging forward to take my mouth in a passionate kiss, our tongues meeting with each swipe as his hand moves into the front of my leggings, sliding through my slickness.

"Yesss," I hiss, and he bites my lip as his middle finger starts gently rubbing my clit until I'm a writhing mess against him. "Please."

"What do you want, Pix?" He kisses my neck, his hand never leaving my pants.

"Please take me. I need to feel you." I pant as my

hips move in time with the strokes of his finger. I'm so close.

"Don't you dare cum until I'm balls deep inside this tight little pussy, Rina."

"Nooo." He chuckles darkly before removing his hand and rips my leggings and underwear down to my knees and undoing his jeans. I moan when he pulls his dick out, the tip glistening with precum before moving to his knees. "Wh—" I gasp as his mouth touches my clit.

He teases me with his tongue, flicking my clit between long and leisurely licks and I cry out with the struggle to not cum.

"Don't you fucking cum, Rina," he growls against me, and the vibrations have my knees shaking.

"I—I can't! Please!" I whine and beg, shaking from the strength it's taking to not cum hard on his tongue and he groans, thrusting his tongue into my entrance.

"You taste so good, Pix. I love eating this sweet cunt." He pulls away, nipping my ass in his teeth before standing behind me.

Wrapping his fist in my hair, he nudges my entrance, thrusting into me hard, making me scream.

"Oh God!" I move my hips back to meet him, taking him as deep as I can, and he grunts.

"You're even tighter like this, unable to spread your legs." He pulls almost all the way out before slamming back in. "God, baby, so good." His hips pound into me while he pulls my hair in his fist.

"Gonna cum, gonna cum, going to-AHH!" I scream as my orgasm slams into me, his thrusts never slowing until he goes over the edge with me, grunting my name as his hips slow to a grind, dragging me through my climax.

"Shit," he curses softly. "You're incredible, Pixie girl," he whispers and I sigh, leaning my face against the hard bark of the tree, trying to catch my breath.

"Not so bad yourself, Sheriff." I wink and he narrows his eyes at me, making me giggle. "Sorry, Daddy. You just fucked me so good, I think I lost some brain cells."

He chuckles hard, slowly pulling out of me, his release leaking out after him.

"That will forever be one of the hottest things I've ever seen." He groans as he watches it trickle out before reaching into his pocket and pulling out a paper towel, cleaning me up.

"Did you plan this?" I ask, half laughing once we're dressed again.

"This? No, but I've learned from our past dalliances that I can't seem to keep my hands off of you, so I always carry something around." He winks, reaching his hand to take mine and I laugh.

"That's a very fair point."

Just as we're getting back to the cabin, Trent pulls up in his truck with Lana in the front seat.

"Boss, we have to go. Carl is on his way back to the main house, but there's been a fire at the Flecher's barn. We need all hands on deck. Everyone is being called out."

He curses beside me before helping me get into the back seat of the truck.

It's kind of this huge thing with four doors and definitely not something I'm used to seeing in the city. But it makes sense for a behemoth like Trent to need something this big.

"What all do you know?" Travis holds me tight while watching Trent for any reaction he gives.

"Not a lot, boss. They aren't sure how it started, but you know how big that place is. They need all hands to try and save as many of the animals as possible."

He curses before looking at me again. "Carl will keep you safe at any cost. Will you be alright without me?" He looks like he'd be willing to say fuck it all if I wasn't, but I refuse to let him risk his job.

"Of course, I will be okay. You trust him, so I know it will be alright." He nods and looks back to Trent when we pull up to the main house.

"How far out is he?" I ask, and Trent looks at his phone before swearing.

"He's having a problem starting the truck, but he says fifteen minutes tops. Think they'll be alright locked up in the house?" Travis pulls me out of the backseat while Trent does the same with Lana. We're just way too short for this type of vehicle.

"I don't like it," he states, and Trent nods in agreement, but Lana and I aren't hearing it.

"Go! It's your job and you need to be there. Carl won't be long, and I promise we won't open the doors for anyone," Lana states, hands on her hips while she stares her man down, and I'm in awe of her.

"She's right. We won't let anyone in. Go do your

job, Daddy. We will be fine." He still looks unde-cided when we all step into the house, so Lana and I square off with them, shoulder to shoulder.

"What are you doing, sweet pea?" Trent growls, and Lana snorts.

"Stopping you two from being idiots. We're completely safe here. Even Ryan didn't attempt to break into the house." I furrow my brows, wondering who Ryan is, but logic points to him being the dead ex she told me about this morning. The one that hurt her, and if that's who Ryan is? Then I say good riddance, asshole.

"She has a point," Trent states calmly. "And we upgraded the system in here since then as well."

But Travis is shaking his head. "Ryan was nowhere near the level of sociopath that her father is." I inhale a sharp breath and he looks at me. "I didn't check into anything more than what my FBI friend sent me, I promise." I release the fear I was holding. "But we know Chad was run out of town yesterday. There's a good chance your father knows where you are, and I just don't want to leave you unprotected."

I take a deep breath and soften at his concern.

"I know, Daddy, but so many animals will die if you don't help." He gives me a sad look and sighs.

"Promise me you will enable this alarm the second we leave, so that the only ones getting in here are Lana's brothers, or Trent and myself?" I nod, and Lana readily agrees.

"We promise. Now go, before it's too late!" Lana practically begs, and I nod my head in agreement while trying to hold back the tears when I think of all the frightened animals.

By the time they're gone and Lana has activated all the necessary alarms, all we can do is sit in the living room and wait.

"I hate fires," I whisper, and she nods.

"Me too, but they will be fine. I know they won't do anything stupid to take them away from us."

I whimper and move closer to her to hold her hand. "I can't lose him, Lana. He's become my everything in such a short time."

She gives me a watery smile and nods.

"He loves you too, you know." I let out a sad chuckle, and she shakes her head. "I'm serious. Before you got here, he was always so serious and working too hard. Trent said he rarely ever left the station. You're good for him." She beams at me, and I give her a tight hug.

"Thank you. I needed to hear that." She goes to answer before we hear a creaking on the stairs.

Exchanging a look, I lean over to whisper in her ear.

"Are one of your brothers home by chance?" She shivers and shakes her head. I pull her into a tight hug, unable to hide my own nervousness.

"Don't ask questions, just text Starburst to Trent and Travis right now, then shut your phone off."

She nods, moving to pull the phone out of her dress while I block the person's view from the stairs.

"Well, isn't this touching." Robert's voice sounds cold and calculated from the stairs, and I feel us both freeze.

Shit, I really hope Lana was able to get that message off. She pulls away from me without looking me in the eyes, turning to my father.

"Who are you? I'm sorry, but I'm going to have to ask you to leave." Her voice is stronger than I know I'm feeling, but she squeezes my hand hard as my father cackles at her.

"You're funny, I like you. It would be a shame to have to kill such a pretty thing." His gaze travels over to me with disgust. "Now, why couldn't you look like a normal woman? If you had, maybe I wouldn't be here to collect you."

I swallow the bile rising in my throat. "You can

do whatever you want with me, just leave everyone else alone."

He snorts and shakes his head, a gun appearing from behind his back that has us both gasping.

"I wish I could make that promise." He pauses, looking thoughtful. "Actually, I don't. They interfered with my business. They've become collateral damage. Though, if you come without a fight, I might be persuaded to tell Chad to back off." I try to steady my heart as it pounds inside my chest, breaking into tiny, shattered pieces as I picture Travis dying because of me.

"I'll go without a fight, I promise," I whisper, trying to stand, but Lana holds my hand with a strong grip.

"I'm not letting you take her anywhere."

Robert scoffs at her while I send her a glare.

"It's cute you think you can stop me, but all that will end up doing is making me kill you. Just because you're blonde and a woman, doesn't mean you have to be stupid."

She gasps, looking at him with disgust, but I throw my hand over her mouth to stop her from saying anything to get herself killed.

"Lana, I know you don't like this but please, shut

the fuck up before he kills you!" I hiss and my father actually laughs.

"Wow, you have a brain after all. Too bad you're worthless to me alive." I close my eyes before letting go of her hand and standing up on shaky legs.

"I said I'd go with you. Just leave Lana here, and we can go." He rolls his eyes at me.

"I'm afraid she's going to have to come with us for insurance. If you do everything I say, I will drop her off somewhere for her to find her way back once I've dealt with you," he sneers and I run over to him, growling with the anger inside of me.

"That's not part of the deal. You said if I went with you willingly, that you would leave her alone!" He raises the gun up to my head, and I stiffen.

I'm not ready to die yet. I'm not ready to die at all.

I want the life with Travis that I've had these past three weeks and I want the chance to finally live my life and be happy.

"And I will stick to that promise, but she can't stay here. There are too many phones and ways she could notify someone before we have a chance to get clear of this godforsaken town," he spits in disgust, and I almost want to smirk at his discomfort.

Almost. You know, if I didn't have a gun to my

head and I didn't feel like my entire world was crashing down around me.

If I wasn't afraid for my life along with the lives of my new loved ones.

"Can I have a minute to go to the bathroom?" Lana asks which has Robert and I both looking at her like she's lost her marbles, before I remember that her brother Carl is on his way.

Is she stalling in hopes that he will save us? Because honestly, I'm more worried about the psycho I share blood with shooting him.

"I don't see why not. I know you're trying to stall for time, but no one is coming for you. Not anytime soon, anyway."

Fear and nausea roll through me.

"What did you do?" I hear my voice shake, and I hate it, but I can feel myself pulling into my shell to try and escape this. Escape him.

"No one is dead, so stop looking so scared. God, I can't believe you ever came from me." He rolls his eyes and waves the gun around a little. "I just simply made sure their trucks wouldn't start while your wonderful ex started the fire to call the other two away."

He looks between us and sneers. "It had to be something big to get them to leave the two of you.

According to Chad, they're always attached to the both of you. It's rather sickening that they've allowed themselves to be demeaned by mere women." He sighs like he's disappointed in the male race. "So yes. If you have to use the washroom, you can, but I will be watching you the entire time." Lana pales and shakes her head.

"Never mind. I'm good." He grabs my wrist painfully while aiming the gun at Lana.

"Disable the alarm so we can get out of here. Do anything stupid and I will shoot you without hesitation." She takes a deep breath and nods before walking to the door and shutting off the alarm system.

"Now what?" She looks at my father with loathing, and I really hope he doesn't shoot her because of it, but he just smiles at her, never taking the gun off her.

"Now? Now we take a walk to my car."

CHAPTER 16
TRAVIS

THREE HOURS LATER...

Now that the fire is contained and we saved as many of the animals as we could, everyone is covered in soot and sweat including Trent and myself.

The fact that we won't know if all the animals made it is weighing heavy on all our hearts, but some of them have bad burn injuries so we just don't know.

"How did this get so out of control?" Trent curses as we watch the smouldering carcass of the once giant barn.

"It's a barn. The second something lit up, everything else was like gasoline to it. Just added fuel to the fire." I shrug, opening the truck to grab some water and my phone.

"Yeah, you're right. I just don't see how a fire could have started in the first place," he mutters, following suit before I almost drop my water when I see a million missed messages and calls.

"What the fuck?" I start sorting through everything, a pit of dread growing in my stomach.

I never have this much activity on my phone.

"Shit!" Trent barks out before giving me a worried look as another truck pulls up behind us with the Easton brothers, and I know it's bad.

"Get in! We have to go now!" Dameon barks from the passenger seat, and that's when I see it. The first missed message was one word from Lana and it's enough to stop my heart beating in my chest.

LANA:

Starburst.

"The girls!" Trent and I both scream at the same time, barreling toward the backseat of the truck with Joe, before Carl drives off like a bat out of hell.

"What the fuck happened?!" I snap at Carl, knowing he's the one that was supposed to be with them, and he winces.

"I don't know. Our trucks were fucked with and when I couldn't get mine figured out, I called these two and they were having the same problems. It was clearly planned to keep us away." I growl and Trent punches the back of his seat. "Watch it fucker, I'm driving!"

"They locked the house when we left. How is it even possible that they're missing? They were safe." Trent is as pissed and on edge as I am.

"What if he was in the house before we left?" I swallow hard as the realization dawns on me. "Is it possible?" I look at Dameon and he shrugs, messing around with something on his computer.

"If he had enough knowledge and know-how, it's possible he could have gotten in when we weren't there. The security measures aren't as tight as I would like them when no one is in the house."

"Where are we going?" I practically spit out when I see we're leaving Haven Hills.

"I'm tracking Lana. They're about an hour outside the town limits."

My stomach sinks hard, nausea and dizziness taking over.

"So, he's had them for hours now?" I try to hold my voice steady.

I doubt he would keep my girl alive that long.

Not unless he has something more elaborate planned than murder.

"According to the security logs, the system was disabled two hours ago. If they're an hour from home, it means he's had them at this location for about an hour," Dameon explains, and the truck goes quiet.

The sick fuck has had them for an hour already and at least a solid half hour more before we arrive, even with Carl driving like the hounds of hell are on his ass.

I don't want to think about the fact that she could be dead. I just need to think positive.

"Where is he keeping them?" Trent asks, and Dameon looks at the computer again.

"A little outside of Clarity." He nods before looking at me.

"You good?" he asks and I scoff. How the fuck can I be good when this asshole has every intention of murdering the love of my life?

"Nope." He nods again with a smirk. "What the fuck are you smiling about?" I snap. "I don't have jurisdiction and if I kill the prick, no one is going to believe it was to save my girl."

He gives me a hard look. "You may not have jurisdiction, but I do." I blink at him. "With Serenity about to open, and me being the go-between, I have jurisdiction from Haven Hills to Omaha. If he needs to be dealt with, I've got your back." My heart starts to race as I watch him.

"I—" He holds up his hand to stop me.

"You saved Lana. It's my turn to repay the favour."

I swallow hard. "But Lana is there too, Trent," I whisper, and Carl snorts.

"He has no plans to hurt Lana," he says, and my head snaps to the front.

"And how would you know?"

Dameon turns in his seat to stare me down. It's not his easy-going personality on show. Right now, he's the hardcore sadist who seeks to bring pain.

It's easy for him to transfer from the willing pain of a submissive, to a less than innocent kind. I have no doubt that he'd be able to kill with ease and easily get away with it.

"Because I watched the security tapes," he says.

"What tapes?"

He lets out a breath. "It's a failsafe we have. Each of us has an app on our phones that can turn the cameras on and off. Lana must have turned them on before shutting her phone off."

They've seriously thought of everything.

"Let me see it."

Rina

By the time we get to Robert's hideout, my nerves are completely shot.

I don't want Lana or Travis or anyone else to suffer because of my messed up past. Not knowing if he's still alive or not is killing my heart.

I'm so close to snapping and lashing out at the asshole who fathered me, and it's bound to happen if he keeps taunting us like this.

Why didn't he just shoot me and get it over with? Why take Lana as insurance?

"Why are we here?" I look to my father for answers, and he shrugs.

"I'm waiting for Chad before I execute the rest of our plan."

Lana is quiet and still beside me. How she's calm and not losing it is beyond me, but she won't tell me what the fuck is going on inside her head. Maybe it's a good thing. There is only so much crazy I can handle at once.

"What's the plan then?" I ask, trying to distract him and myself.

He looks at me for a long while. I'm not sure if he's studying me or what he's doing, but his face is a statue. There is absolutely no emotion to see.

"I suppose I could tell you. It's not like you'll be able to tell anyone from the grave." His eyes travel over Lana. "But she could. Unless I kill her too. She's awfully pretty, though. Maybe I will keep her as my own toy."

Lana chokes a little and I watch her from the corner of my eye, but she does nothing.

"Leave her out of your sick and twisted games, Robert."

He pretends to gasp, grabbing at his chest where his black heart resides. "Is that any way to speak to your father?"

He's got to be joking. I can't stop the humourless laugh that falls from my lips. "Right. The father that loves me so much he wants me dead. That one?" His face turns dark, and he walks up to me. I don't even have time to react before pain shoots through my face.

"Shut your mouth, you little bitch!" he seethes.

"If my parents weren't such stingy fucking assholes, your pathetic little life wouldn't matter, and you could have lived." He straightens himself before glaring down at me. "I thought getting rid of them was all I had to do to get the rest of their money, but no. They had to put it in their will that I had no control over your trust fund." He gives me an evil smile. "If you want to blame anyone for your impending death, blame them."

"You...you killed them?"

He cackles hard, the evil more evident than I've ever seen.

"Your grandfather was easy. He always wanted to see the good in people, even when it didn't exist. My mother however, was much harder. She was suspicious of me for years. It took a lot of time and convincing, not to mention money, to pay someone she trusted. Good riddance to that selfish bitch," he spits, and I can't stop the tears from falling.

Lana bundles me up in her arms as they fall harder while Robert laughs at the sadness he created.

"How can you be such a monster?" Lana cries out to him as she holds me tight, and my father snorts.

"I'm no monster, sweetheart. Well, not that

you've seen." He comes over and pulls her off me before grabbing me and ripping me off the floor and onto my feet. "This is me being a monster." He pulls back and punches me in the stomach half a dozen times before throwing me on the floor, leaving me in a heaping coughing mess.

"What the fuck is wrong with you?!" she screeches, running toward me, but he pushes her away before his boot connects with my chest and I hear a crack.

"You wanted to know the plan, Katrina?" he shouts as his kicks meet my stomach and chest until I'm coughing up blood.

"St—op," I croak and he laughs. "Please," I beg.

He kneels down on the floor beside me, holding up the gun before giving me a dark smile.

"Don't worry. You won't feel a thing." I feel a sharp pain through my skull as Lana screams before everything goes black.

CHAPTER 17
RINA

Everything hurts when I try to move, and I let out a pained groan.

"Oh my God, Rina!" I hear Lana cry out before I feel her beside me.

"Lana," I croak as pain shoots through my skull. "You need...you need to get...out of...here." I gasp as pain shoots through my chest when I take a deep breath.

"Try to take shallow breaths. I'm pretty sure he broke a couple of ribs." She leans over me and whispers in my ear. "The guys will be here soon, I promise."

I shake my head and wince. "No. N-not possible," I whisper and sag back onto the floor of the basement he has us in.

"It is. Trust me, okay? They will be here soon, just hold on. If you die, I'm going to bring you back to life so I can beat your ass myself." She sounds so serious that I let out a chuckle before moaning in pain.

"Don't do that." I try to smile, but she snorts.

"Sorry. I'm just scared. I thought he killed you. I kept watching your chest to make sure you didn't stop breathing."

Shit.

"How long?" It's all I can force out, but she must understand.

"At least a couple hours, babe. Just try not to move," she tells me, and I cry out in pain when I try to ease the pain in a different position. "I just said don't move! Geez, woman!" she scolds me.

"Sorry," I hiss as I bring my knees into my chest and lay on my side. "It...hurts."

She huffs out a breath and grumbles. "He's lucky he went upstairs right after he beat you. I almost clawed his eyes out. Such a donkey prick."

"Ugh, don't make me laugh, you bitch," I groan, and she giggles before I hear sniffling.

"Sorry. I just hate men who think that hitting a woman is okay and vice versa. It's never okay to hit someone, let alone beat them bloody." I fight to open my eyes and the light peering into the room sears into my brain, making me shut them again.

"He's never done this before." It must be a part of his plan to kill me. He's never cared enough to beat the shit out of me this badly before.

"He'll never do it again either."

I hope she's right.

Travis

If we don't reach the destination soon, I'm going to lose my temper.

I've kept it together for the last forty-five minutes of the drive, but only just. Watching the surveillance footage of that prick holding a gun to Rina's head has me on edge.

For all her fear, she didn't cower, and I am so fucking proud of her for that, but I'm not an idiot. This was going to haunt her for a long time, and she'd most likely need Derek's help on a constant basis.

Deciding to distract myself while the others are gearing up, I give my brother a call.

"Hey, Travis. I'm a little busy at the moment. What can I do for you?"

I wince. "Just giving you a heads-up and calling in a favour with my little brother."

He mumbles something before I hear a door close. "Alright, I'm alone. What's going on? Heads-up about what?" His concern is genuine, and I hate that we don't talk much. He's my little brother, after all.

"Remember me asking about Borderline Personality Disorder a few weeks ago?"

"Yeah?"

"It was for my girl."

"Your girl..." He trails off. "You have a girlfriend with BPD?" I nod even though he can't see me.

"I do, yeah. It's fairly new, but she's the one." I swallow down the emotion making my voice crack.

"Okay... well, I'm happy for you. Is that the heads-up you wanted to give me?" I let out a slow breath before pinching the bridge of my nose to calm myself.

"Not exactly. Look, there's a lot of shit that I need to explain, but she's been through hell. Her father and ex are trying to kill her to gain her inheritance." He sucks in a breath, but I keep going. "They've kidnapped her and Lana. According to the surveillance tapes, he has no intentions of hurting

Lana, but he needs Rina dead, Derek. I don't know what we're about to walk into."

He's silent for a split second before I hear him shuffling things around.

"Alright. I'm catching the next flight out. Do me a favour and don't let anyone but Evans talk to her?" I nod. "Are you listening?"

"Shit, sorry. I nodded but forgot you can't see me. I'm losing it right now, brother." My voice cracks and he keeps going.

"You're there to get her now, right?"

"Yeah. We tracked Lana with the earrings they got her last year."

"Good. When you get her, I need you to keep her as calm as possible. There are a million different ways she could react to this stress, but the one thing you need to do is make sure you don't leave her side. She's going to need your comfort and may come across as needy for a while."

"I can do that. The last time she got even remotely stressed, she kind of became a zombie for a while, then when she came out of it, she was very Little. Like, almost baby, little. I'd venture a guess of maybe two years old."

"She's a Little?" he asks, and I let out a harsh breath, worried he's going to judge me.

This is the side of ourselves where we tend to differ on things. He doesn't understand being a Daddy Dom.

"She is." My voice is guarded, and he curses.

"I didn't mean it in a bad way, but if that's how she handled it, you're going to need supplies. What does she like?" Confusion runs through me as Trent hollers that it's time to get moving.

"I have to go but uh, she likes robots. And she sucks her thumb when she's that little, and when she sleeps."

"Okay. Okay, I can pick up a few things. My flight leaves in two hours. I will be there as soon as I can. Send me updates when you have her."

"Thanks, Derek. I owe you," I say before hanging up the phone and silencing it, so it doesn't go off at the wrong time.

Walking back to the guys I look to Trent.

"Derek is on his way. If Lana needs him after this, he will be here."

He nods and gives me a look of determination. "We're getting our girls back." He looks between everyone else. "Remember to try and let me do the shooting if it's possible."

We all nod before heading towards the house

that Robert is keeping the girls in according to Lana's tracker.

I need to get one of those for Pixie the second I can.

Once we get close to the house, Trent waves his hand for Dameon and I to take the front door while he, Carl, and Joe head off to the back to stop anyone from leaving and we give him a nod, splitting up.

As I go to knock, I hear someone screaming inside before something is thrown against the wall by the door. Sharing a wide-eyed look with Dameon, we draw our guns to be safe before stepping to the side. I quickly knock my knuckles off the door.

"What the fuck took you so long, asshole? I should shoot you where you stand!" the voice bellows and Robert opens the door to be met with our guns trained on him. "Oh, fuck off." He holds up his gun to shoot us before Carl steps up behind him, pressing his gun to the back of his head.

"Not so fast, asshole. I have a few questions for you." Trent comes around his other side and takes the gun from Rina's father who is fuming. His face is red and blotchy as he tries to control his anger.

"Go to hell," he spits through his teeth, and I smirk at him.

"That spot is reserved for you, you worthless

piece of shit." His face gets even redder as the four of them fight to get his arms and feet zip tied before dropping him on the couch.

"You kill me, and you'll never find them," he sneers, and Dameon bends down to look him directly in the eyes, a coldness on his face that even has Robert flinching.

"How do you think we found you?" He shakes his head like he's disappointed in the prick. "I expected more from a supposedly ruthless mastermind such as yourself. You didn't even do your research, did you?" Dameon sneers at the man and he narrows his eyes back.

"I don't have any idea what you're talking about." Robert seems to calm down after that, almost like he's back in control. When I share a look with Carl, I know I'm not the only one who notices it, but we say nothing.

I want to see what he has planned.

"Right." Dameon stands back up. "See, I did a little digging of my own. Both of your parents died of a heart attack a few years apart." I watch Robert's face as Dameon tells him everything he already discovered about the guy.

Apparently, Trent figured Dameon would be able to get the information without it being traced back to him. He hadn't wanted to get my hopes up before they had any solid information.

I'm going to have to remember he's some computer genius for future reference.

"Your point?" He acts almost bored, and I keep my hand on my gun just in case.

"They were old enough, sure. The thing I found suspicious though, is you refusing to allow them to autopsy your mother." His face turns slightly red again as Dameon continues. "Did you know your mother had an autopsy performed on your father? Course, she had a private lab do the procedure, so it didn't wind up in the police files." Robert is shaking with anger. "Poison."

"You son of a bitch!" Robert lunges for Dameon, his arms coming free from behind him, but he doesn't get far.

Between the ties on his feet and the bullet Trent puts in his shoulder, he crashes to the ground, screaming in pain.

"That wasn't very nice," Dameon taunts him, clucking his tongue. "Don't worry. The feds are already building a case against you. Your days of being a free man are over."

I watch on in glee as the blood pools on his shirt. His shoulder is going to need rehabilitation for sure.

"I'm going to read him his rights. Go get the girls." Trent shoots a look at me, and I nod, heading towards the basement while Joe heads upstairs and Carl guards the door in case someone comes to the house.

Rina

"Did you hear that?" Lana hisses, and I groan.

I'm in and out of consciousness from the pain and I'm pretty sure I have a concussion from being pistol whipped since I can't seem to pry my eyes open for more than a few seconds at a time.

The marching band in my skull playing at horrendous levels is also a dead giveaway.

"What?" I groan and then I hear it. Slight muffled shouts upstairs and my heart rate picks up in fear. "Oh God, he's here."

"Who?" she asks because she can tell I'm afraid rather than relieved.

"My ex. He has to be the one here. There's no other possibility." A little of me dies more inside knowing I won't ever get out of this alive. The only thing I can do is pray that Lana will.

"Not true." She's calm and has been almost this entire time. Aside from when I took a beating, she's been pretty chill about this whole thing and it's starting to piss me off. Does she have a death wish or something?

Fuck, maybe she's insane. Would fit the bill that the first real friend I've ever had is even crazier than I am.

"Lana." I wince when I try to move and open my eyes, but I fight through it anyways.

"No, Rina. Trent, Travis, and my brothers are here. I know it's them making all that noise."

"How?" I try to not get my hopes up, but she seems so damn positive now that I'm looking at her.

"Because my earrings have a tracker in them." I blink, not even knowing how to respond to that. "After my ex almost beat me to death," her voice breaks a little, "and then started stalking me, the guys had these made for me in case Ryan ever got his hands on me again." She shivers. "After he did get me, I decided to never take them off." She lets out a calming breath. It's clear the trauma she went through runs deep.

"So...they're coming for us? There's hope?" I croak, and she nods as the door to the basement busts open, making us both scream. "Oww," I groan, the pain taking over everything else.

"Pixie! Pixie, are you in here? Lana!"

"Here!" Lana screams, then winces when I flinch. "Sorry. We're safe. I told you they'd find us." She smiles down at me but I'm too focused on the blurry image of Travis coming into view.

He runs over to me as Lana moves out of the way. Kneeling in front of me, he gently cups my cheek.

"I'm right here, Pixie girl. I've got you, baby." It's the last thing I hear before the world goes black.

CHAPTER 18
TRAVIS

I can hear voices outside of her room as Trent talks to the officers that were called in to arrest Robert.

When I walked into that basement and saw my Pixie girl laying broken and beaten on the floor, I wanted to murder him, fuck the consequences. The only thing that stopped me was knowing Rina needed me more than that asshole needed to die in that moment.

Between Trent having jurisdiction and Lana being able to tell the officers everything that happened, I know we're all in the clear anyways.

The only question they still had was why we hadn't called it in.

I'm not proud of it, but I lost my shit on them at

that. Rina was in surgery to stop some internal bleeding they found in her abdomen, and I had run out of fucks to give to anyone that wasn't her.

Thank fuck Trent pulled me back and calmly explained to them that we had an extremely stressful day with the fire, and we acted on instinct when we got the emergency text from Lana. After they heard that, they backed off so I could panic in peace.

Now it's been almost twenty-four hours since I got her back, and she still hasn't woken up. The doctors are positive she's going to be fine and say it's the concussion keeping her asleep. That the trauma her body sustained due to her piece of shit father has caused her body to go into a form of hibernation. Rest is what she needs to heal so that's what her body is giving her.

"Fuck, baby. Please, wake up," I whisper, squeezing her hand as a knock lands on her door before Derek walks in. "You made it."

"Yeah." He looks at my girl, and I can see the sadness and anger rolling through him before he turns back to me. "How's she doing?"

I shrug, turning back towards her. "Doctors say she will recover, but she hasn't woken up yet." My voice cracks and he's beside me in an instant, resting his hand on my shoulder.

"She needs some time to heal. Physically and mentally." I nod. "Has she shown any signs of nightmares yet?" he asks, and I shake my head.

"No, not yet."

"That's a good start. It's going to take her time to heal, Travis."

I growl. "I fucking know that. God! When I saw her on that basement floor, I thought she was fucking dead, Derek." I shake my head of the negative thoughts and run my free hand down my face. "He beat the shit out of her."

He squeezes my shoulder. "I talked to Trent before I came in here. I got the rundown of her injuries. She's a fighter."

I actually smile. "She's the sassiest, most infuriating woman I have ever met." I chuckle. "She's also the bravest."

"I love you too, old man," she croaks from the bed, and I jump up.

"Oh, thank fuck, Pixie! I was so worried. Can I get you anything? Are you thirsty? Do you want Circuit?"

She groans. "Too many questions." I shut the hell up fast and Derek smiles. "Water please."

"Of course." I grab her cup of water and bring the straw to her mouth. "Here, baby. Can you open your eyes?" She struggles for a few seconds before opening them and blinking at me.

"Hey, handsome," she greets me in her joking tone before opening her mouth to drink.

"Slow." I guide her, making sure she doesn't get sick from drinking too fast.

"I'm going to let Evans know she's awake." Derek squeezes my shoulder before leaving.

"Who's that?" she asks once she's finished drinking.

"That's my brother, Derek." She scrunches up her nose, wincing. "What hurts?"

"Everything." She swallows hard. "I don't remember a lot."

I nod in understanding. "You had a really bad concussion. Doctor Evans said you may have memory lapses."

"Maybe that's a good thing," she whispers, her eyes filling with tears. "Lana. Is she okay?"

"She's fine. Pissed off about everything he did to you and will be shaken over being kidnapped again, but she's working through it with Derek. She's going to be more than fine."

Her tears spill over, and I grab a tissue from the

table by her bed. "Does she hate me now?"

I pull back in shock. "Never."

"I'd hate me."

"This wasn't your fault, Pixie girl," I tell her the truth, and she snorts before wincing.

"Yeah, it is. If I had never come to town, you'd all be safe." I feel the anger bubble up in me but keep my tone as even as possible.

"I will never be sorry you came into my life, and I damn well know Lana feels the same." I take a deep breath. "This was your father's and Chad's fault. No one else is to blame for their psychosis."

Her face pales as fear flashes in her eyes and she squeezes my hand hard. "What happened to them? Where are they?"

I grunt, not sure how much to tell her, but she deserves to know everything.

"Your father is in jail without bail until they can get a hearing to sentence him." She opens her mouth, but I hold up my free hand and keep going. "He's already pleaded guilty to some of the charges. Enough to keep him locked up for a really long time."

"What?" She's confused and I get that.

"He's caught on camera taking you and Lana at gunpoint, so he's confessed to the kidnapping, but there are a lot of things Dameon has brought to light. The feds are looking into a lot of other charges right now, so everything else is just on hold until further notice."

She looks like she's contemplating asking what the other charges are, but I hope she doesn't. Her brain needs time to heal before worrying about all of that.

"And Chad?" she whispers his name, and I sit on the edge of her bed, bringing both her hands into my lap.

"We haven't found him, but he's most likely dead."

She squints. "Why do you think he's dead?" she asks and I wince, feeling nauseous just thinking about what my officer Ethan and the fire department Chief had told me.

"Do you remember the fire that called Trent and I away the day you were taken?" She nods. "Well, they found a body in the horse stall where the fire started. Preliminary scans showed excessive trauma from the horse panicking. Best guess is that whoever started the fire was trampled on while the horse was scared, before they broke free." I see the way her body relaxes when I say the horse broke free and it makes my chest ache.

Even after everything she's been through, she's still worried about an animal she's never met.

"So...the horse killed him?"

I blow out a breath. "We haven't gotten the reports back on who the person is, or if they were dead before the fire or not." I shrug. "I'm pretty sure they will match the dental records to your ex. Whether he died from being trampled or burned to death, we don't know."

She takes the information and rolls it around in her brain as Derek and Doc Evans walk back into her room.

"Rina, it's good to see you awake." Doc Evans smiles at her and I narrow my eyes, but don't say anything.

"Hey, Doc," she greets him and returns the smile, but hers is guarded.

"How are you feeling?" He eyes the glass of water that's now empty and she sighs.

"Everything hurts and I don't really remember much."

He looks over the machines hooked up to her before writing some things in her chart.

"I can get you some more pain meds in a moment."

She smiles a genuine smile this time. "Yes please. Thank you."

He smiles back at her. "Anytime, darling."

I growl at him, and Rina looks at me like I've lost my mind.

"Did you just growl?" Her eyes are wide. "Why did you growl at the doc? Do you need to sit down? You look a little flushed," she points out, and I narrow my eyes at her.

"I'm fine." I look at Richard, my long-time friend. "Mine."

He smirks at me, and Pixie reaches out to swat me before wincing.

"Ouchie," she grunts, her voice going small, and I soften a little.

"Did you just hit me?" I ask.

She rolls her eyes, and I can see my brother shaking from the corner of my eye. "Duh. You were being a giant meanie ogre again."

Derek actually starts cackling from the corner and trying to catch his breath, so I glare at him before turning back to my sassy girl.

"Again with the mean ogre? What did I ever do to you?" I pout and she giggles, softening both Richard and my brother with one sound.

"Glad to see you still have your fiery spirit, Rina,"

Richard says before getting back down to business. "As far as your memory loss goes, it's not uncommon after a head injury. Especially when said injury occurred during emotional trauma."

Pixie swallows and reaches for my hand to squeeze. "Will I remember what happened to me?" Richard looks between us before focusing back on her.

"You might, and you might not. You could also have flashbacks come out of nowhere, but never fully put the pieces back together."

"Should I ask Lana to tell me?" She glances between Richard and Derek now and my brother steps to the end of her bed.

"That may be something to look into at some point, but your brain needs the rest more than anything else right now."

She nods in understanding. "Why does my stomach hurt?" Richard gives her a sad smile.

"You sustained some really bad injuries and had some internal bleeding in your abdomen that required surgery."

Her breath catches. "What else?" Her voice wavers, but she holds eye contact with him, refusing to shy away from this.

"On top of the internal bleeding and severe

concussion, you have a few broken ribs and a frac-tured cheek bone." Her hand reaches to touch her face and she winces.

"I must look like shit." It's barely above a whis-per, but I hear it.

"Katrina Flemming! You will not talk down about yourself. You're always beautiful and I will not let you belittle the woman I love."

Her bottom lip wobbles. "Sorry, Daddy." I give her a firm nod before leaning over to gently kiss her lips, making sure to not hurt her.

"You're everything to me, Pixie girl, and you will always be beautiful both inside and out."

"I love you too," she whispers, giving me a sweet smile and I kiss her again.

"As sweet and touching as this is, Rina needs to get her pain meds and rest. I'm going to send a nurse in with those soon. Rest up Katrina." He pats her shoulder gently before leaving.

It takes less than ten minutes for the medication to knock her out, but not before she asks for Circuit. As I sit here watching her snuggle up to him while sucking on her thumb, I send Trent a thank you text for him and Lana thinking to grab him for her.

CHAPTER 19
RINA

SPENDING A WEEK IN THE HOSPITAL WAS THE LAST thing I wanted to do, but the doctors wouldn't let up. Not even under Travis' intense glare.

He was too on edge having me here because I was on edge. I hated that I set him off like that, but I wasn't comfortable being around a bunch of people, and with how much pain I was in I desperately wanted to go Little and couldn't. No matter how much he promised to safeguard her, it just wasn't doable for me in my mental state.

Trust is something I will always struggle with because of my BPD, and he understood that.

Which leads me to now, sitting on Travis' couch and having a stare off with Derek.

"How are you feeling now that you're home,

Rina?" He's being nice and sweet, but it's hard to fully register that this is home for me.

It doesn't feel real. Just like it's hard for me to trust people, it's also difficult to believe in a good thing when it happens.

"I don't know," I whisper, playing with the blanket on my lap rather than looking at him.

"What don't you know, exactly?" Gah, I hate psychiatrists and therapists—really anyone that tries to get inside my head. But this is my Daddy's brother and he's trustworthy. Even Lana told me how much he has helped her over the past year.

"I'm not used to good things being real."

He makes a sound, but I can't place it. Pity? Sadness? It's always the same. Everyone feels bad for the poor broken head-case.

"With everything Robert has put you through, that doesn't surprise me. Can I ask you a question?"

I lift my eyes to watch him. "Like I really have a choice in the matter."

He looks taken aback. "You always have a choice, Rina. I'm here to offer some help while you start to process everything, but you by no means *have* to talk to me." I watch his face to see the lie, but it's not there. He is one hundred percent being truthful. If I told him to get fucked, he would.

So, I decide to try. If he's being honest about wanting to help, then I can give it my best shot. "Sure. Ask away."

He nods, shifting in his chair. "Do you trust my brother?"

"More than anything." I feel the heat burning the back of my eyes, but I've cried so damn much this past week, I'm seriously over it.

"So...if you trust him and what you have, then wouldn't it stand to reason that you could trust that this is your home now?"

I draw in a breath, readying myself to explain what goes on in my head, positive he will be like all the rest. He just won't get it. "Logically, yes. Mentally though?" He waits for me to continue as I try to gather my thoughts. "Mentally, I've never had anyone stick around just because they want to. My mother left when I was little, my father killed my grandparents, and my ex was working with him all along. I've never had anyone."

"You know about him killing your grandparents?" He looks surprised and I blink.

"Uh, I...yes but I don't know—" My memory flashes to a dark room with Robert taunting me with their deaths while Lana was sitting beside me. "He told me when he took us. I didn't realize I remembered any of it until now."

"Do you think you remember anything else?" he questions.

I try and focus on that piece of information, the feel and sounds of the room in my mind, but nothing solid comes back, just fragments of emotions.

"I-I can't remember details. I remember feeling angry and betrayed when he confessed that, and I remember pain, but I don't remember him causing the pain."

He pauses. "That's normal. You may never remember all of it. Our brains have a sort of failsafe to lock away certain things that happen, so we don't wither and crumble. It's a way to protect us from ourselves."

I sigh, going back to playing with the blanket. "That's what Doc Evans said that first day. Well, sort of."

He smiles a bit. "You're right, he did. Do you want the memories to come back?"

I shake my head so hard I actually get dizzy. "No. Definitely not."

"That's okay, too. I can't promise they will stay locked away, though. Anything could trigger a memory to surface, you just have to be prepared for that."

"I know," I say, barely above a whisper.

"Getting back to the original question topic then, what else is going on mentally?" I whimper as another vision comes to me.

I'm lying on the floor in pain as the butt of the gun comes down towards my face and I can't hold back the scream that flies out as I curl into a ball, covering my face with my hands.

No.

No this isn't happening again. He's gone from my life. I can't let him destroy me like this when I'm finally safe.

"I can't!" I hear myself wail, but I'm no longer in charge of my own mind and body. "Daddy!"

I feel myself starting to rock as footsteps rush into the room before strong arms surround me.

Travis

Hearing a scream that rocks me to my core, I rush back into the living room where she's sitting with Derek just before she screams, "Daddy!"

I look at my brother who's already standing by her, trying to issue words of comfort but he won't touch her, and I thank fuck for that as I move in to help my girl.

"Hey, Pixie girl, it's alright I've got you," I coo in a soft voice before moving to gently lift her into my lap. "Shh, baby, it's okay. Daddy is right here. You're safe, baby, you're safe," I repeat over and over again, rocking her in my arms as I ignore the pain starting in my lower back from the repetitive movement.

"She had a couple flashbacks. The first one didn't trigger her so whatever this one was, I assume it had to do with the beating. She tried to guard her face." He swallows hard as he watches me rock my baby girl. "What can I do?" He looks lost and I wrap my arms around her tighter.

"Grab her robot off my bed? She needs him." He nods, heading towards the back of the cabin.

"Daddy, please don't let him hurt me," she whimpers, and I have to hold my anger in check. I wish I could kill the bastard for hurting her like this.

"Shhh, baby. No one is ever going to hurt you again, I promise."

Derek comes back a few moments later with Circuit and hands him to me. Pixie instantly pulls him to her chest before shoving her thumb in her mouth, and Derek makes a sound that has me looking up at him and I see longing in his eyes.

He wants a baby girl? That's new. I don't mention it though because I know him. He will tell me when he's ready.

He reaches into the bag in his hand and pulls out a large pacifier before handing it to me and shrugging when I give him a questioning look.

"I told you I was going to grab some things you may need." He nods to the thumb in her mouth. "Does she know she does that?" I sigh into her hair as she starts to snore softly, making us both chuckle.

"I don't know. I've never asked her, but I should." I reach for the pacifier and look at it before smiling.

There's a winking robot face on it and it's actually fucking adorable. "Hey, Pixie girl." I tug on her thumb a bit and she whines, her eyes fluttering open. "Do you find comfort sucking on your thumb, baby?" I ask and she nods.

"Yes, Daddy." She blushes and I beam at her.

"I think it's super adorable, Pixie girl." She sighs in relief and goes to pull it back in her mouth, but I stop her. "Do you want to try this?"

She opens her eyes again and looks at the pacifier for a solid minute while we wait for her response.

Derek had moved away from us so he wasn't in her line of sight. He didn't want her to be worried that someone else was seeing her so vulnerable and I appreciated him for it.

"Okay, Daddy," she whispers, and I open the little case it came in and guide the paci into her mouth.

After a few trial sucks, she lets out a contended sigh and closes her eyes to drift off back to sleep.

"Want to show me what else is in that bag?" I whisper to Derek, and he smirks.

"Just an adult sized bottle and a robot dining set with sippy. And maybe some fun robot bibs and a onesie?" I give a quiet chuckle when he actually blushes.

"Thank you, Derek. For everything." He just plops back into the chair across from us and leans forward with his elbows on his knees.

"She's going to have these flashbacks for a while, I think." He watches her sleep, sucking on her paci while cuddling into me with Circuit.

"I know. Any suggestions?" He coughs, clearing his throat before moving his gaze back to me. If it were anyone else looking at her like that, I'd probably sucker punch them, but I know he's just trying to figure out his own desires, wants, and needs. If he's looking for a Little, it's completely new territory for him.

"Just do this and be there for her. Don't leave her alone for a while unless she strictly asks for it and even then, don't go far." He takes a deep breath. "Trauma survivors often get triggered easily and without knowing everything he did to her…" He shrugs his shoulders. "I'll talk to Lana and see if I have her permission to give you the full run-down, so you can more easily identify what could be a trigger."

I nod, pulling her closer.

"That would be good." I grind my jaw as we sit in silence, thinking of ways we can help her.

EPILOGUE

Rina

THREE MONTHS LATER...

I'm going to strangle him, I swear to God.

I get that I've been healing, and I've had a few terrifying breakdowns that have worried the hell out of him, but I need space.

I'm seriously thinking going full on escape mode is my only option at this point and I know it's going to end in a spanking, but I need this, and I will gladly take the punishment.

The second he goes off to the bathroom, I grab my purse and practically run out the damn door. It's

241

not like it will take him long to find me with this tracking necklace I always wear.

Hell, there isn't even a danger to me anymore.

My father killed himself after he landed in jail for the rest of his life because Dameon handed in the proof that my grandparents died of less than natural causes.

On top of those murder charges, he was charged with kidnapping as well as assault and battery. They wanted to press for attempted murder charges, but he wasn't trying to kill me when he beat me, so they went with their next best option—intent to commit murder.

When all of the charges were thrown against him, he decided to take his own life, but not before leaving me a nasty letter that Travis never let me read.

Not that I really wanted to hear or see any more of his hateful words towards me.

My useless scumbag ex got exactly what he deserved too.

After a few weeks, it was confirmed that it was his body recovered from the barn. He had so many broken bones from being trampled that it was a miracle he hadn't died instantly. The reports showed charred lungs which meant he died in one of the most painful ways possible.

I know I shouldn't be so gleeful about another person's suffering, but he was trying to kill me for a payout like my life meant absolutely nothing to him. Then add on the fact that he was almost responsible for dozens of animals dying and I just can't find the sympathy.

"Abigail Davies! Get your ass back here!" I hear shouting across the street and feel anxiety trickle through me, but I take in a few deep breaths so I don't let it win, and then look towards the yelling.

"Fuck you, D!" I watch as a young girl, maybe sixteen or seventeen, gives Dameon Easton the finger before running away from him.

Looking both ways to make sure it's clear, I cross the street and greet a very angry man.

"Hey, Dameon. Everything okay?" I ask, and he blinks down at me before sighing.

"It's fine. The little shit just stole my sweater from my truck."

I gasp. "Ummm…"

He narrows his eyes at me. "You shouldn't be out alone, Katrina."

I growl at his use of my full name. I've come to

prefer Rina since Robert insisted on calling me by my full name. It's just a memory I'd rather forget.

"You know what? I'm glad she stole your sweater and I agree with her sentiment a little." He raises his eyebrows in shock.

"You're in so much trouble for that, Pixie girl." I hear Travis behind me and groan.

"Oh, come on! Couldn't you have at least given me a few more minutes?!" I stomp my foot, throwing my hands up in exasperation and Dameon gives me a dark smile.

"No." I feel his arms band around my waist, and my traitorous body leans back into him, making him chuckle. "You are going to have a very hot ass when I'm done with you tonight," he whispers into my ear, and I shiver.

"Need any help with discipline, Sheriff?" Dameon taunts, and my eyes widen before Travis' arms pull me tighter.

"Nope. No one touches her but me, but thanks for the offer." The asshole cackles before nodding his head and walking away. "You're lucky I didn't take him up on that offer, Pixie girl."

"W-why?"

He gives me a feral sort of grin. "Because, baby. He's a sadist."

"Daddy, I promise I will never ever do anything bad ever again!"

He chuckles and laces his fingers with mine before we head back to the station. "Pixie, I don't believe that for even a second." I huff out a breath and he boops my nose. He actually booped my nose in public!

"Did you seriously just boop me?!" I gasp, and he smirks.

"You're damn right I did."

"God, you're infuriating for an old man!" I stomp back into the station with him hot on my heels.

"Hmm, I've changed my mind. I know just the punishment for you to show you just how *not* old I am."

I freeze in my tracks before turning to face him. "No, I'm good. I'd rather the spanking."

He shakes his head. "No, Pixie. Tonight, I'm going to fuck you for hours with my tongue, fingers, and cock and you won't be allowed to cum until I say so." He moves into my space until we are right against each other. "And when I say hours, I truly do mean hours. Get ready for edge play as your punishment, baby."

He gives me a quick kiss before walking to his office laughing.

"You're going to let me cum at some point though...right?" I squeak, and he shrugs.

"If you're a very, very good girl and beg so sweetly, I will let you cum before bed." I sigh in relief and his eyes darken. "But you better be prepared to sleep all day tomorrow because that orgasm? The one you'll be begging for? It's going to wreck you."

Oh shit.

THE END

Please subscribe to my NEWSLETTER for any updates on when the next books in Serenity Stables are being released!

DADDY'S PRECIOUS ROSE
SNEAK PEEK

Suited Up Daddies 4

Lena

Five years ago...

Sitting in the living room with Dad, I can tell he's lost in his own world again.

He gets this distant look in his eyes while he stares into space. It's a sure sign he's lost in thought.

I know he's thinking about the past because I'm turning eighteen in a couple of days and getting ready to start college. I even got a full ride scholarship but chose to live at home instead of the dorms because it's my comfort. The one and only place I've ever felt safe because of my past.

I first met George when I was five years old. He came onto a crime scene to rescue me from a bad situation like he was my own personal knight in shining armour.

I can't sit here and tell you it wasn't as bad as it seems, because it was.

A couple of men had broken into my childhood home in the middle of the night and murdered my parents in cold blood before taking me as ransom. If they had known that there was no one else in the world to claim me, I would have been killed alongside my parents.

When they took me from my home, they locked me in a large closet with my hands tied behind my back before closing the door and leaving me in the dark. I had no clue how long it would be before they figured out that I was a burden they didn't want, but I knew it would always end in my death.

I'm not sure how long I was there before George and his team found me, but I do remember not wanting anyone to come near me when they finally opened that door.

Imagine being a five-year-old kid locked in a

dark room and hearing loud shots ringing through the air. Scary right?

I wouldn't let anyone near me when they opened the door to that closet. How was I to know if they were good or bad people?

I screamed and cried and kicked until George walked into the room. Something about him felt warm and kind and I knew without a doubt that he wasn't going to hurt me. For the first time in hours, I felt safe. When they realized they couldn't tear me away from him without traumatizing me farther, they let him stay with me.

Day in and day out, he never left my side, and it wasn't long before he quit his job as an officer and opened a PI firm so that he could legally adopt me as his.

He kept me safe and loved instead of throwing me into the system and forgetting about me like so many would have done.

I know that's where his mind is at now as I watch him over the edge of my book.

"You're doing it again Dad," I tell him, shaking him out of his thoughts.

"Sorry, kid. Can't get anything past you, can I?" He chuckles and I shake my head with a smile.

"You know better than to try." He nods and I stand up to give him a kiss on the cheek. "I love you, Dad."

He nods as tears well up in his eyes.

"Love you too, sweetheart." He pats my shoulder. "Go and get changed. Ford leaves tomorrow and he invited us over for dinner tonight." He smiles at me and my heart rate picks up at the sound of his name.

Ford Wallace.

Shit, even his name was sexy.

He's been Dad's best friend as long as I've known them, and from how they tell it, they've always been inseparable.

"K." I run up the stairs to get ready and throw myself on the bed, trying to talk myself down.

A part of me, an immature part, is mad at Ford for leaving because I have been in love with him since I realized what that even meant.

He's the guy I compare everyone to which is probably why I have never dated anyone my age. Even thinking about it makes my skin crawl. They're too immature and pathetic for me to even consider when I have someone as smart and handsome as Ford to compare them to.

It's a tough order to measure up to two of the greatest men I have ever known.

He's never shown an interest in me aside from being his buddy's little girl, but I am feeling his move as a loss just the same. I'm losing a friend and one of the only people I have known most of my life and it's a hard pill to swallow.

I just wish he would see me as anything other than the child I used to be. Instead, I wish he saw me as the woman I've become.

<hr>

Ford

Packing up the last of my things, I glance at the time. George and Lena were going to be here any minute.

Growing up together in Charlotte, Georgia, I can't remember a time when we weren't friends even though we've always been polar opposites.

I was the book nerd who loved to learn while he was more into sports than school. I was tall and lean with black hair while he was shorter with blonde hair and muscular from the sports he played.

Even our personalities were the opposite. Where I was always cold and distant, he always cared about people and saw the best in them. He made friends with everyone while I stayed a loner.

He was, and always has been, a man with a bleeding heart. He loved to love and help others with whatever they needed even if that meant giving them the shirt off his own back. I guess that's how he ended up being a father to Lena.

Not that I can complain about that. She has made him happier these past thirteen years than I have ever seen him. It's like she breathed the life back into him that his job had taken away. There's only so much bad you can witness before some of your soul leaves with it, and that's exactly what happened to George before he found his daughter.

I was never one that enjoyed being around kids, and it only got worse as the years passed, but I didn't mind Lena too much. She'd had a rough start to life. She was quiet and liked to keep to herself and every time I saw her, her head was always stuck in one book or another.

She was a cute kid.

Was, being the operative word. Once she hit fourteen and started high school, George and I ended up way beyond our comfort zones. I had to hand it to him though, he handled the teen years like a pro.

Now that she was eighteen and getting ready to start college, calling her a kid didn't seem to fit anymore. She had grown into a beautiful, independent and strong woman who was smart as a whip. She was even smarter than a lot of the adults I come across on a daily basis.

Looking around the barren rooms of the place I had called home for the last fifteen years, I couldn't believe I was moving away from my hometown. I'm forty years old. I figured I would always live here.

I never imagined my security company would take off and get so much business that I would be opening offices across the US, but that's just the way life happens sometimes.

Wallace International Security had started out as a brain child of mine back in business school.

My main goal was to open an office in Savannah, about forty minutes from Charlotte, and provide top of the line security guards for events in and around the neighbouring areas.

It was a gap that had needed to be filled, but as the business grew, demand became more popular for other services that members of my team were able to provide. As mainly ex-military, they were tough and sharp. Before I knew it, we were offering services across the United States and even accompanied some people overseas on their travels.

The office in Savannah just wasn't big enough to

run as home base anymore. So, after extensive research, my board and I settled on Chicago as our new, larger base of operations. The office here would remain open but would handle more of the planning side than the physical operations.

I also chose to move because I was starting to see Lena in a way that made me sick to my stomach. She wasn't a kid anymore, but she was still my best friend's kid, and I was more than twice her age. It just wasn't right and there was no way I was willing to risk my friendship over some odd attraction I may have felt towards her.

Before I can dive deeper down that black hole, the doorbell rings pulling me out of my thoughts.

Opening the door, I greet them.

"Hey. I'm glad you guys could make it. Pizza should be here any minute. Come in." I move aside to let them by and as Lena passes me, her arm brushes against my front and I stop breathing.

What the hell was that Ford?! Get your shit together, you idiot.

Before I could figure out what that reaction could mean, the pizza arrived.

Perfect timing too. I didn't need to be trying to dive into the recesses of my brain to figure that shit out.

After dinner, we moved into the living room where George and I talked while Lena played on her phone and tried to pass the time.

Every once in a while, I would catch her glimpsing my way and when I did, she would blush and lower her gaze back to her phone.

Over the years, as she grew older, it was fairly easy to see that she had a childhood crush on me, but I wasn't too concerned about it. You almost always grow out of them, and she never tried to act inappropriately towards me, so I ignored it.

"I can't believe after forty years in this town, you're leaving us behind for bigger and better things!" George says laughing.

"Neither can I if I am being honest. Once I hit thirty, I assumed I was going to die here. Single and alone." I chuckle and take a sip of my scotch. "Not all of us can have everything we ever dreamed of, right?" I nod my head toward Lena, and George smiles.

"Yeah, she's a dream come true. She completed my life in a way I never imagined, you know?" The love in his eyes is unmistakable as he watches her sleeping on the couch with her headphones in.

"Ah hell, man, people in this town are so stuck up. You can still fall in love you know. I mean, you got the kid you never thought you would. Anything is possible." At forty-three, there were only a small handful of people in his life that he trusted enough to be around.

George loved people, but after Lena became a part of his life he stopped trusting so easily. People assumed he didn't have time for dating because he spent most of his life working to advance within the police force, and then when he became Lena's adoptive father, he was solely focused on raising her and building his own PI business.

They weren't wrong, but his main concern was someone else coming into his life and then leaving and that destroying Lena. She had been through enough in her life already and he didn't want her getting hurt again.

"Yeah, I know. I'm not a monk, but no one has ever been good enough to possibly bring that kind of crap down on her. It's just too much drama. I'm content with what I have and taking care of her is everything. She's my life."

I nod in agreement.

Marriage and kids had never been on my radar, but he was the definition of a family man. I focused on my business and casually dated here and there but it never went anywhere. That was the one and only area where George and I were similar.

One night stands, no complications.

"Looks like you should get sleeping beauty home to bed," I tease as we both stand up.

"Yeah, she's not the most fun to be around with little sleep." He laughs as he shakes her awake.

She wakes up slowly to take in her surroundings before standing up and wiping her eyes. "Sorry, Ford. I didn't mean to fall asleep. Thank you for dinner."

"Not a problem. Thank you for coming. Take care of your old man when I'm not here, alright?" I chuckle and slap George on the back. It's not like I was never seeing them again, it just wouldn't be nearly as often.

"You got it!" She laughs as they're walking out the door.

I shook hands with George and said my good-byes as they started towards their car, but before I could close the door, Lena jumps into my arms and gives me a giant bear hug like the ones I would watch George give her when she was little.

Taken by surprise, I stumble back a bit before

catching my balance to stop us both from falling over and she giggles.

"I'll miss you, Ford," she whispers in my ear before dropping back to the ground and walking away with a little wave and smile.

'God, I'm gonna miss you too.' I think to myself as I watch them drive off.

Walking back into the house, I have no idea where that thought came from. Sure, she was kind of like family so I would miss her, but this didn't feel like that. This felt different, but I couldn't place it, so I chalked it up to being exhausted and then headed to bed to get ready for my early departure tomorrow.

AFTERWORD

Whew! This book was another emotional ride for me, but I loved every second of it.

Travis and Rina have been in my head for months, yelling at me and demanding their story to be told and they were none too happy about being made to wait haha.

When the idea for the Serenity Stables series came to me, I knew I wanted it to be different than my other books. I wanted each book to address something real that many people struggle with and so far I've chosen things I personally connect with.

There's always a story behind someone's smile, and mine hasn't always been the happiest.

What Rina goes through as an individual with BPD is some of my own personal experiences with it, but is in no means how it affects everyone.

Like I said in the preface, if you've met one person with BPD you've met one person. We're all different and unique with our own stories to tell.

Thank you so much for taking the time to read these stories and I hope they help bring you some joy. <3

ACKNOWLEDGMENTS

First and foremost, I want to thank the readers who have given me a chance and fallen in love with the characters in my head.

I love writing about Daddies and their Littles and I have no intentions of stopping :).

Always, thank you to my husband for being supportive and understanding as I lose sleep because my brain won't shut off and more characters and ideas come to play!

My best friend and cover designer, Jade I fucking love you every single day! None of this would be possible without your belief and support.

My beta team of readers, you guys are the bomb dot com and I love your input! Thank you!

ABOUT THE AUTHOR

Cassie Hargrove is an emerging author of all things romance. She is a stay at home mom to 3 children. Twins age 8 (both have severe autism) and a sassy and rambunctious 5 year old.

She is a photographer in her spare time and lives with her husband, kids, dog, and 3 cats. She has been writing most of her life and recently chose to share that love and passion with the world.

   Writing brings an element of calm in the chaos that is life.

ALSO BY CASSIE HARGROVE

Suited Up Daddies

1: Daddy's Naughty Secretary

2: Daddy's Little Novice

3: Daddy's Proper Present

4: Daddy's Precious Rose

5: Daddy's Sexy Sub

6: Daddy's Perfect Pair

Box Set with Bonus Novella

Serenity Stables

1: Healing with Daddy

2: A Home with Daddy

3: Rescued by Daddy (Coming Soon)

Connerton Academy

(A College Paranormal Why Choose Romance)

1: Freshman Firsts

2: Sophomore Secrets

3: Junior Justice

4: Senior Sacrifices

The Revenge Diaries

(A Series of Dark/Very Dark Standalones)

1: Trick or Revenge

2: Beautiful Revenge (Original and Less Triggering Versions)

3: Love's Dark Revenge (Coming Soon)

Standalones

Depravity: An Extremely Taboo Novel (Co-Write with Seven Rue)

The Art of Freedom and Growth (A Depravity Extended Epilogue) (Co-Write with Seven Rue)

The Deadly Seven

A Co-Write with Story Brooks

1: Obsession

2: Seduction

3: Devotion

4: Salvation

5: Justified Retribution: Kristen's Story (Coming March 2023)

Dark Series

1: Dark Torment

2: Dark Longing

3: Dark Adoration (Coming Later in 2023)

Erotic Shorts

Taken By Him

Intern-al Affairs

Bound To Him

Santa Daddy's Naughty Baby

CASSIE HARGROVE WRITING AS A.L. RYAN

Standalones

Roommates: A Dark Sapphic Romance

Forbidden Kinks

Book 0.5:

Still His

Previously Published as Still by Cassie Hargrove

Printed in Great Britain
by Amazon